STILL UNDER FIRE

Paranormal Investigative Services
Book Two

Sheri Lyn
Cassidy K. O'Connor

This book is dedicated to our mom, Patti. When she first saw the title, she thought it was going to be some gross serial killer stuff. Boy, was she not wrong. Regardless, as any good mom would, she sat with us for way more hours than she probably wanted to and painstakingly went over the medical scenes with us. It helps that she has been a critical care nurse for our entire lives. We promise to make the next book way less complicated.

To Shane, we are eternally grateful for your brilliant plot lines and willingness to talk through the holes. Keep those great ideas coming!

To Dr. Brumfield. Thank you for taking the time on a Saturday to talk us through some of our medical questions. We will be ever grateful that you didn't even hesitate when we mentioned the victim was a salamander shifter. Your excitement at discussing how the procedure would be slightly different in our fiction world really made our day.

Author's Note

Author's Note: If you picked up this book, it's because you want an escape from reality. This is a world where people turn into animals. Some fly and others breathe fire. We spent many hours with an Internal Medicine/Cardiology Physician and a critical care nurse trying to make the medical side of this story as accurate as possible, but we had to take some liberties. We ask that you suspend reality with us and just enjoy the story.

PART
One

CHAPTER

One

"THIS IS Sicily Bronson with ABC Action News on the scene in Downtown Tampa where a paranormal fight resulted in catastrophic damage to humans and infrastructure. We have an eyewitness here to describe what happened."

"I saw the whole thing. I was sitting in the cafe over there drinking my coffee. That's when it all started. Darkness overtook the street, and the roars echoed down from above. The sound gave me goose-bumps all over my body. Then suddenly a long tail swooped down, barely missing a couple walking." The witness pointed to a spot on the other side of the road.

"The creatures were in a battle to the death and it was obvious they didn't care who they hurt in the process. The dragon, at least I think that's what it was. It looked nothing like they do in the movies. It dug its talons into the minotaur's back." The man imitated the claws wrapping around a large body.

"The minotaur screamed so loud the windows actually shattered, glass went everywhere. People were screaming as they got cut up from the flying shards. Next thing you know, the dragon had opened his claws, and the Minotaur was falling to the ground. That's when I saw the chunk of the leg missing from the minotaur."

The man paused as he blew out a breath and focused on a spot outside. "It crashed to the ground, crushing vehicles and smashing the windows of the buildings as it went. The dragon followed after it, blowing fire. That's when a small car turned down the road and slammed to a stop. The minotaur grabbed the dragon by the throat and pinned it to the street, blocking the car's path. I thought maybe it was over then, you know." He licked his lips as he glanced back at the reporter as tears filled his eyes.

"The dragon blew a fireball into the minotaur's face, sending him backward. Then they ran at each other as the dragon blew out another fireball. They crashed into one another and were thrown on top of the car. The dragon stood first, slamming its tail on top of the car, repeatedly trying to crush the minotaur. And then it was as if the whole world froze but for the screaming coming from inside the car. The dragon grabbed the minotaur in its claws and flew away with it. There was nothing left behind but silence."

"Well, I think everyone would agree we're glad to see you are safe." Sicily turned back to the camera. "There's a press conference scheduled later today with more details, but preliminary estimates are coming in with at least five dead, and another fifteen injured. The most critical patients were sent to Tampa Medical Center. The property damage is expected to reach the millions. We're told a manhunt is still underway for the responsible parties."

CHAPTER

Two

MADDOX GRABBED the last gallon of paint out of Tristan's truck and hauled it inside.

Tallie, the teenage ex-prostitute currently staying with his mother, squealed as she saw the dab of color on the lid. "My room is going to be insane. You guys are the best."

She skipped down the hall. Maddox let out a deep breath.

"You guys spoil her, and I think that's awesome. She deserves to have the room she never had as a child." Marta, Maddox's mom, patted his shoulder affectionately.

He had to maintain an air of grumpiness, but deep inside, there was nothing he wouldn't do for the girl. If she wanted her room to look like she lived in an actual tree with a waterfall flowing around it, he would have found a way to make it happen. Lucky for them, she only asked for a forest mural. Tallie had grown up with an abusive father until she ran away to live on the streets. She didn't deserve the hand dealt to her. His mom offering to take the girl in to help with her own loneliness was the perfect fix.

"Hey, Marta," Tristan called out with a twinkle in his eye. "You know our new apartment isn't decorated yet. Your son is being no help with colors. I keep telling him he's gay, he should have a say, but he's as stubborn as the day is long. What's his favorite color?"

"He always loved fuchsia."

Maddox gagged. "Absolutely not. Nothing should ever be painted that shade of disgustingness. I will be so pissed if I come home and my living room is now that god awful color."

Tristan laughed. "I noticed you didn't specify if it was pink or purple. I swear some of those combinations confuse the hell out of me."

"Stop flirting and get in here and work on my room," Tallie yelled from down the hall with impatience.

"Geez, didn't take her long to get comfortable

bossing us around," Maddox grumbled as he hustled down the hall.

"Something tells me with her former line of work she learned how to read what people like... as in you taking orders ...."

Maddox glared at him over his shoulder. "We both know there isn't a submissive bone in my body."

Tristan threw his head back in laughter as he trailed after his partner down the hall and into the teen's bedroom. "So... we didn't talk about this before, but I can't draw. And unless you're hiding that ability from me.... We may not have thought this through completely."

Maddox cocked his head as he stared at the empty wall. "Um Tallie, how good of a job are you expecting? If it ends up looking like a kindergarten class did it, would that be okay with you?"

"Grandma," Tallie screamed in alarm as she raced toward the door in wide-eyed terror.

Maddox bit back a grin. It sounded so weird to hear her call his mom grandma. It was sweet, but weird.

Marta popped her head in. "You already have a problem? You haven't even started."

Tallie waved her arms violently toward Maddox

and Tristan. "These two agreed to the mural and just now admitted they can't actually draw."

Marta smiled broadly. "You know... your dad is a fantastic artist. What if he comes over and sketches it all out? All you guys have to do is paint between the lines."

Maddox's stomach did a little flip. His relationship with his dad was tenuous at best and his relationship with Tristan was still hovering around first base. Was he ready to have them meet?

Tristan's eyes bugged as he slowly raised his hand to gain their attention. "I'm not sure I'm ready to meet the 'rents. That's like a year long relationship milestone. Not like I met your son a couple of months ago and moved in together last week."

Marta cocked an eyebrow at him. "I'm a 'rent as you call it and you've already met me. I feel like chopped liver. You're only worried about meeting his dad?"

"No... well shit." He grumbled as he moved to hide behind Maddox. "That's so not how I meant that at all. But I can see where I went wrong. And now I'm just making it worse with my blabbering. Maddox, help me out here."

Maddox crossed his arms over his chest. "How dare you offend my mother, in her own house."

Tristan gaped at his sort of boyfriend. "You Judas. If we shared a room, I'd kick you to the couch for that."

Tallie gasped. "Oh my god. You guys sleep in separate rooms?"

Maddox looked at her, then over at his mom. This was not a conversation he wanted to have with either of them.

Marta held a hand up to stop him before he could respond. "As much as I too would love an answer to that question, I know better than to expect one from you. I'll call your dad and see when he's available."

"Your son has decided to take things slow with me. My virtue is intact I'll have you know."

Tallie scrunched her eyebrows together. "Wait, I thought Maddox was some kind of man-whore?"

Maddox rubbed his eyes. "This just keeps getting worse. Can I die now and avoid all of these conversations?" He sighed and looked back at Tallie. "Not that it's your business, but both of us had thirty-six plus years of prejudices and hatred to get past. He was a human six weeks ago. That's a big change on its own, let alone starting a relationship, too." He looked back at Marta. "Cover your ears for a second." He turned back to Tallie. "Trust me, I want to obliterate his virtue. I just thought taking it slow was good for him."

"And now I sound like I was complaining when I was only making a joke at your expense. But he's right Tallie. I'm not quite ready to go there yet. I've gone through some major upheavals and it's changed my whole world. That being said, I've been into guys since I knew what my dick was for. So I appreciate a gorgeous guy when I see one." He winked at her as he heard Marta snort from behind him.

Marta pulled out her phone. "I'm going to save my son from any further embarrassment and call his dad." She pulled out her cell and hit a button. "Silas, your son needs you. How soon can you be here?"

The air in the room thinned seconds before a portal opened and his dad stepped through. "I'm here. What's wrong?"

Every jaw in the room was open. Maybe he shouldn't be surprised his dad came so quickly, nevertheless, it shocked him. He didn't really have a relationship with him, so why would he come running to his aid?

Marta recovered first and slid her phone back in her pocket. "Well, that was efficient. Thank you for coming."

Maddox could swear her face was red. Ewww.

Silas scanned the room. "I think there are a few introductions that need to be made?"

Maddox pointed to Tallie first. "This is Tallie. She is a friend that needed a place to stay and mom offered to let her live with her for a while." Silas nodded at the girl then looked expectantly at Tristan. "This is, uh... Tristan... my partner."

"Partner on the force..." Tristan offered a wave and then winced... "Uh... and um... we just started dating, too." He grimaced and looked at Maddox. "I freaking panicked and didn't know what to say." He whispered loudly.

Silas walked up to Tristan and stood inches from him. For a long minute, he just stared at him. Maddox was about to intervene when Silas reached forward and gave Tristan a hug. "It is wonderful to meet you." He stepped back and over to Tallie. "And I suppose I'll be seeing a lot of you now that you're living here."

Maddox swung around to Marta. How often was his dad over for booty calls?

She definitely was blushing this time. "Anyway. We called you over because it turns out these two offered their services for something they can't even do."

Maddox's phone buzzed in his pocket. He saw the call was from Vic, their boss at P.I.S. "Excuse us a second." He waved at Tristan to follow him out into the hall.

Maddox answered and put the phone on speaker. "Hey Vic. What's up?"

"Remember when you called in the other day after the near destruction of Downtown Tampa and I told you not to come in, we had it handled? Well, we just had a body drop that needs our attention. I know you two are off for another day, but I really need you to come in."

"Not a problem. You are saving us from a very awkward situation anyway. Be there in an hour." Maddox hung up the phone and popped his head back into the bedroom. "We got called into work so unfortunately we have to go. We can make plans to meet up again to work on the mural if you want?"

Silas was already drawing on one wall. "You two go ahead. Marta and Tallie are in excellent hands."

Maddox shuddered. Now that he knew his parents still hooked up, he was horrified on a whole new level. He was never so happy to go see a dead body.

CHAPTER
Three

TRISTAN STAYED quiet as they drove to the office. He couldn't get the morning out of his head, mainly meeting his partner's father and making an ass of himself. "Hey man. Why didn't you ever mention how fucking gorgeous your father was? I could have been so much smoother if I'd been fore-warned. But no, he just popped in and I froze. He's a total Silver Fox."

"First of all, you knew he was Fae, so automatically it's a given they are good looking. Second, who says their parent is gorgeous? That's just weird. Do you say your mom is hot?"

"Uh, she might have been once upon a time. But time and her illness have taken a toll on her." Tristan shrugged as he pulled into a spot. "Is it wrong to say

I can see why your mom has a thing for him? You take after him a bit though too."

"Am I going to have to keep you away from him? Do I need to worry about some daddy fetish you might act on?" Maddox shot back as he got out of the truck.

"Wait... is that a possibility? Does he bat for our team too?" Tristan held up his hands in an I surrender gesture and laughed. "Just kidding. I swear I was just teasing you. Trying to lighten the mood a bit."

Before Maddox could respond, Vic opened the door to their pod area with a folder already held out. "Glad you guys could dress for the occasion. We have a werewolf found in an alley in Ybor and I'll save what's special about it for when you guys get there."

Tristan looked down at his casual house work outfit, "We have a change of clothes in our office here. Figured we could kill two birds with one stone and stop here before going to the crime scene. If you want us to go home first, we can do that..."

Maddox pushed past them toward their office. "Dude Tristan. He's just giving you a hard time. Get your clothes, we'll check in with the team, then head out."

Vic smirked. "Do we need to have someone monitor the locker rooms while you guys change? Time is of the essence, after all."

"No worries there. We live together now. We can behave ourselves at work." Maddox smiled cheekily as he grabbed a gym bag from his desk.

Tristan groaned as he reached for his own tote. "Dude, stop saying shit like that to him. I don't care what relationship you have with him. It still freaks me out that he's our boss. I'm still the low man on the totem pole and I need this job."

Maddox ignored him and stopped at the table in the center of the pod. Ensley and Sheppard were staring at a laptop. "Hey guys. Any progress made on your case?"

Sheppard sat back and blew out a breath. "It's been eight days and we still don't have these assholes in custody. We've identified them, but they seem to have disappeared."

"We still have four people in critical condition, too. These guys really fucked up." Ensley said as she pushed away from the table to grab a pastry from a box behind her.

"Knowing who they are is something though, they can't hide forever. You'll get them." Tristan reassured them.

"Well, if you guys need someone to be a sounding board, let us know." Maddox held up the folder Vic had handed him. "In the meantime, it appears we got a mysterious body to go check out."

Ensley glared. "Oh sure, rub it in. You guys are going to do something fun."

Sheppard elbowed his partner. "That is so morbid."

Tristan nodded in agreement with him as he gestured to the door, "We gotta go change. We'll see you guys later."

Some days he really questioned the mental stability of people in this line of work.

Tristan and Maddox flashed their badges at the Tampa PD cop, then ducked under the police tape.

"I really hope Judd is the forensics tech on this one. You haven't met Bruce yet. Guy is a fox shifter and is just as shifty as a human. Judd is great though. Super nice and goes out of his way to help in any way he can."

The tech in question stood up and turned to wave them over. He held his hand out to Tristan. "We haven't met yet. I'm Judd."

Tristan smiled and accepted the handshake. "Hey."

Judd grinned, "I've heard a lot about you. Gossip runs rampant around the office. Add in that you've apparently tamed the untamable and you're already a legend."

"He got to you too?" Tristan groaned good-naturedly.

"Nope," Judd winked, "Actually, we're just friends. I knew his reputation before I joined P.I.S. and no matter how charming he is, I resisted. It was difficult, but I did it."

Maddox grunted, "You aren't even gay."

"Not necessarily, but I didn't slam that door closed. If the right person came along, who knows what would happen." Judd grinned and waved to an officer standing off to the side. "He was the first on the scene. We've already taken his statement. He didn't have much to offer, though. He claims not to have disturbed the scene or touched the body. There was no way the guy was alive, so he just called it in."

Tristan cocked his head. "Why were we called in over his forensics team? From here I can't tell that he's a paranormal."

"If you step to the side a bit, you'll see his hand has partially shifted." Judd explained as he pointed,

"He moved back to the opening of the alley and kept it blocked until more units could arrive to hold the scene. It's basically been untouched until we arrived with Sabrina a few hours ago. We're actually getting ready to take the body once you guys have had your look around."

"Did you find anything of note?" Tristan asked as he took in the markers littered around the dirty alley.

Judd laughed sarcastically, "It's impossible to tell what's of use and what's the usual garbage left here on a normal day." He turned and waved. "Sabrina, you have a minute?"

"This is our M.E. Dr. Sabrina Zanders. Doc, this is the agency's newest recruit, Tristan James."

Sabrina smiled and offered her hand. "Sorry we're meeting under these circumstances, but I've got to tell you, this is one odd case."

"Yeah, Vic mentioned there was something weird about this one," Maddox mentioned as he walked closer to the body.

"You could say that. We won't know everything until we get him back, but it appears the only thing wrong with him besides most of his blood being on the outside of his body is that it looks like his kidneys are gone. You can see two incisions on either side of the abdomen."

"I'm sorry. Did you say his kidneys are missing?" Maddox bent down and looked closer at the gashes.

"Neat right? You hear about this stuff on T.V. but I've never actually had a case like this." Judd said a little excitedly.

Tristan was going to add him to the list with Ensley and their questionable mental stability.

"The time of death was between four and eight a.m. yesterday. I'll do an autopsy immediately and let you know what else I find." Sabrina nodded at them and walked away.

"Did he have a wallet or anything to identify him?" Tristan asked Judd as he squatted down to get a better look at the body and the surrounding area.

"Yes, it's bagged up already. His name is Mark Sequoia. He lived a couple of blocks from here according to the address on his license." Judd handed over the evidence bag. "That's all I know so far."

Tristan nodded and stood up. "You seen enough?"

"Yeah, let's get back and start looking into who might want to kill Mr. Sequoia."

"Hey Judd, can you send us the photos you guys

have taken as soon as you can?" Tristan requested as he glanced around one more time.

"Sure thing. We'll be bagging the body in a moment and then I'll get them uploaded to the system so you guys can access them by the time you get back to the office."

Tristan paused and turned back to face Judd. "Who took the officer's statement? Has anyone set up a canvas of the area?"

"Tampa PD is handling that part. The officer's statement is already written up and uploaded as well. We were on scene for a bit before you guys were sent out. We were just waiting for you to see the scene before we finished up."

Maddox shook Judd's hand. "You're a rockstar as always. See you later." He caught up to Tristan on the way out of the alley. "You know... Mrs. Diaz's food truck is two streets over. We can get some lunch to take back to the office?"

Tristan's stomach growled at the thought of her delicious food. "Hell yes. It's a date."

"Speaking of dates. We need to go on a real one soon. I'm free tonight if you are?"

"You don't know my schedule? It's not like I've been far from your side since the day we met." Tristan laughed and shook his head. "The only thing

I have planned any time soon is going to visit my mom. It's been a few days since I saw her." He hesitated. "You're welcome to come with me sometime if you want. She's not always lucid enough to know me, but some days I get lucky."

Maddox mock gasped. "I thought it was too soon to meet the 'rents." His smile dropped. "In all seriousness, though. I would love to meet her."

"Don't worry, she'll love you. Anyone that has her baby boy's back is good in her book."

Maddox reached across the truck cab and pinched Tristan's cheek. "Oh, her baby boy. That is freaking adorable. I'd ask if I can start calling you baby boy, but I really don't want to feed into that daddy fetish."

CHAPTER
Four

MADDOX ADJUSTED his tie four times before the waiter came over to get his drink order. Why he was nervous about going on a date with Tristan was beyond him. In truth, he couldn't remember the last time he went on a date, but that wasn't it. It was because of who it was with and the very real feelings he was developing for him.

He took a large swig of the beer the waiter had brought, then saw Tristan at the door. He'd never seen him dressed up before. The man looked delicious in a suit. He needed to talk to Vic about making suits mandatory at the office.

He waved to get his partner's attention and adjusted his tie again. He had to stop doing that.

Maddox stood as Tristan neared, then leaned

forward and awkwardly kissed his cheek. He felt like such an idiot. "You look great. You still think it's weird I had us meet here like a real first date?"

"There isn't anything normal about our situation or relationship, so it threw me off a bit. What was really weird was waiting in my room for you to leave, so I didn't see you dressed up. It felt like Christmas when I was a kid. You know when your mom is wrapping presents and tells you to stay away."

"Well, maybe if you are good at dinner, I'll let you unwrap me later." Maddox gulped. Had he really just said that? He was more than ready to take the relationship further, but that sounded like he wanted a home run right away.

"Can I ask you a question without you making fun of me for once?" Tristan took a sip of his water as he waited for a reply and to build his courage to ask.

Maddox adjusted his tie again. "Absolutely. Like I said, I want this to be a proper date, so I promise to be on my best behavior."

Tristan laughed, "Ah yeah, okay. So, in the books, you know how they have fated mates. Do paranormals not really have that? Do writers just do what they want and ignore reality?"

"We have true mates. We know immediately when we've found our person. This is the one we plan to spend our lives with." He took another swig of beer. "Since you brought this up, I'm just going to put this out there. I do believe you are my true mate. I have no doubt. But I know we have a lot of hurdles to get over, so I am in no rush to force this. And if you don't feel the same way, that's okay. A lot of times in books they say if fated mates aren't together, they die. That isn't real. It just feels that way."

"So... how do you know I'm the one for you? And it's not weird that we're totally different... um... Species? Also, is that why you slept around so much? You didn't want to get attached to someone who isn't your mate?"

"When I look at you, every fiber of my being tells me you are mine. It's as natural a thought as breathing is. You are mine. As for species, people cross breed all the time. That's how you get ligers and pegacorns. Yes, that's a thing. We haven't even ordered and we are talking about some serious shit." He laughed awkwardly. "So, I don't think I was intentionally avoiding relationships. I just didn't really see the point in investing in a relationship that I knew wasn't permanent."

Tristan nodded in understanding, "So if you know I'm yours, that means you're mine, too. Why don't I have those same thoughts? I mean, don't get me wrong, I feel a connection to you, and I definitely lust after you, but I don't look at you and scream mine. Or is it your paranormal side that does that and since I'm still learning to work my side, it's not developed..."

Maddox shrugged. "I think that's a question for Dr. Obinski. But in my opinion, humans don't feel as strongly as paranormals do. I feel like they don't see colors as bright, or tastes as strong, so it's not a surprise your connection to your feelings aren't as strong. Then again, I did have to smack your ass to make your wings pop out, so I'd definitely say you haven't fully connected with that side of you. Could be that." He smiled cheekily and took another sip of beer.

"Maybe I just like a little bit of pain," Tristan smirked as he turned his attention to the waiter, who appeared beside them with a twinkle in his eye. Tristan gave him his order for a drink and then glanced around the restaurant before meeting Maddox's eyes again. "So, the case today."

"Uh uh. No work. I don't care how awkward this conversation is. We are on a date, for god's sake. No talk of bodies and murderers when we're trying to woo each other."

"Woo?" Tristan bit his lip to keep from laughing. "Okay, grandma."

Maddox glared at him. "It sounded right at the time. Now accept my wooing, damn it."

"Weirdest date ever." Tristan winked. "But probably the best too."

Maddox leaned forward. He could feel his cheeks heat up. "This is truly my first real date. I know I'm butchering this, but I really am trying to do what you are supposed to do on a date."

"Babe," Tristan leaned forward so they were only a couple of inches apart. "Fuck the rules. We already live together and have been in each other's pockets for weeks. We just need to focus on what works for us. Don't get me wrong. I love the idea of going on dates, but I don't want either of us to feel pressured. I like you. You don't have to impress me."

In for a penny, in for a pound. Maddox was going full disclosure while they both had all their defenses down. "Trust me, I haven't even started impressing you yet. When we do finally sleep together, you are going to be seriously impressed. I am that good and I dream about it every night."

Tristan cocked his head and studied Maddox. "I guess all that practice is going to work in my favor one day. Should I plan a parade in your honor or maybe a party?"

Maddox reached across the table and grabbed Tristan's tie, using it to pull him closer. "Trust me, I really am that good. No parade or party could be too small to celebrate the feelings I'm going to give you." He gave him a no-nonsense kiss and sat back.

"Based on the fact you have groupies, I don't doubt it. It's funny though, I got the impression that you were afraid to take that step with me. Like you thought it would scare me off or something. Half the time I made a comment or innuendo and you back-tracked. The other half you came on like a mack track. Until you finally told me you were in that day on your couch, I really didn't know what to think. I'm so freaking attracted to you it's insane. But at the same time, my head is... was saying hold up." Tristan shrugged and paused. "It's just a weird situation, I guess."

"The cheeky answer is, I am two parts of a whole. The ogre side of me backtracks and the fae side of me is a hornball. But the real answer is, I'm a man-whore whose never been in an actual relation-ship and, of course, I finally meet my true mate and the fucker is a baby paranormal who hated our kind six weeks ago. My heart and my head are constantly warring. Well, my dick is also in this war and it often tells my heart and my head to shut the hell up and take you, but out of respect for your situation, I am doing my best to try to be good." Maddox wanted to throw up. He'd never been so honest before, and he hated it. He didn't like admitting he had flaws and that made him sound like a complete fuck up.

"Please don't take this the wrong way, cause I'm not sure I know how to say it without it coming out badly. But I don't look at you and see a paranormal. I see you as a sexy ass man who makes me laugh and cares about me. I forget you aren't human, you know."

"Out of respect for my kind, I take that as an insult." He winked at him. "I'm declaring here and now, I want you. I'm ready when you are. We'll take it at your pace. Just know that I'm doing my best to be a good boyfriend but I'm in no way perfect, so I apologize now for my mood swings."

Tristan gaped at Maddox in shock, "Boyfriend? You're okay with labeling us like that? I mean, in my head, that's what I called you, but I didn't want to tie you down to something if you weren't ready for that title."

Maddox waved over the waiter. "Can you get us a

bowl of ice cream with a candle in it? I want to celebrate with my new boyfriend."

Tristan laughed as he grabbed his phone from his pocket with a grin.

"You are taking your phone out at a time like this?" Maddox looked incredulous.

"Yes, hell yeah I am." Tristan winked at him and then went back to typing. "I'm googling how many dates are appropriate before sleeping with your man."

Maddox threw his head back and laughed loudly. "Can you give me five minutes before you do that? I'll call Cole and tell him to hack google so it says it only takes one date. Which for your information we are technically on so we can check that off."

"Actually, you'd be wrong about that." Tristan waggled his eyebrows. "We had a date for lunch this afternoon at Mrs. Diaz's food truck. I even said it's a date, and you didn't say no..."

"Well, hot damn. If Cole does his job, then I am going to be getting lucky tonight. This really is a celebration worthy of ice cream."

This was not at all how he thought the date was going to go, but he was really glad they cleared the air. Now he just had to survive the massive case of blue balls he had until Tristan was finally ready.

CHAPTER
Five

TRISTAN FOUND himself whistling as he drove the short distance back to the apartment he shared with Maddox. They'd only just moved in a few days prior, so the place was still in a bit of disarray, but it already felt like home. It was a huge change from his motel room and Maddox's one bedroom he'd had previously. As he pulled his truck into his designated parking spot, he saw Scarlet already there. Did Maddox do ninety the whole way to beat him home that quickly?

As he headed into the building, he took in the parking lot and surrounding area for anything suspicious or out of the ordinary. The way his life had been going the last few months, he figured he couldn't be too careful.

"Honey, I'm home." He called out with a laugh. "Man, I had the best date ever tonight. He's gorgeous, funny, and so into me you wouldn't believe it."

Maddox leaned against the wall, his ankles crossed. "Oh really. Should I be jealous?"

Tristan smirked as he sauntered up to Maddox until he was standing inches from him. "Nah, you get to reap the benefits." He stepped back and winked. "I'm going to my room to put my gun away real quick."

"But what if it's your gun I'm interested in?"

"Didn't your momma teach you not to play with a loaded weapon?"

"In my experience, the loaded weapons are the most fun."

"Fuck it," Tristan groaned as he pushed Maddox against the wall. He enjoyed the look of shock in Maddox's eyes. He ran his hand up Maddox's chest to his head and gently pulled his head back, exposing his neck.

"What are you doing?" Maddox asked breathlessly.

"Shhh." Tristan grazed his lips against Maddox's throat. "You are so fucking hot and driving me crazy." He trailed kisses across his jaw, avoiding his mouth.

Maddox growled. He liked that he was frustrating him. It was going to make everything that much hotter when it finally happened.

He gently sucked on his neck as his other hand trailed down to Maddox's groin and cupped him through his pants. "Someone's already ready for me?"

"You have no idea." Maddox panted. "Kiss me. Please."

Tristan bit his lip and smiled. "You're so fucking sexy when you're begging me like that."

Maddox shoved Tristan back against the opposite wall and then grabbed his wrists and held them above his head. "Don't get used to it. I don't beg. I plan to tease you until you are begging to come. And only when I think you're ready and deserve it will I let you."

Tristan whimpered and licked his lips, "Gods, yes. I can't wait to feel you inside me. The only question I have now is your bedroom or mine?"

"Mine," Maddox grinned, "My bed is bigger." He grabbed Tristan's tie and headed down the hallway with him in tow.

"So fucking hot when you're demanding like that."

"Good, then it'll make things easier when I tell you to strip and get on the bed before I rip your nice suit off you."

Tristan gasped, "This is my best outfit. You wouldn't dare."

Maddox growled as he spun around and pushed Tristan up against the wall of his bedroom. "I'm not a man who denies myself things I want, until you. My patience is hitting its limit and now that you've agreed to be mine, I'm done waiting." He loosened Tristan's tie and pulled it from around his neck. "Am I going to have to undress myself when I'm done with you, or are you going to help push things along?"

"What if I want you to do a striptease for me?" Tristan licked his lips as he pushed Maddox back a step and unbuttoned his own shirt. "Show me what you got, big boy."

"Next time. I'm too impatient." Maddox growled as he undid a couple of buttons before ripping the shirt over his head and tossed it on the ground.

"Fuck that's hot." Tristan whimpered as he let his own shirt drop and started working on his pants.

Maddox grinned as he grabbed Tristan's arm and

pushed him towards the bed. "Time's up, get on the bed, baby."

Tristan didn't waste time arguing as he stumbled forward with his pants around his ankles. He spun as he reached the bed and sat down. "Not to ruin the moment, but I need to get my shoes off if this is going to work."

"Why do I find that sexy as hell?" Maddox questioned as he toed off his own shoes and then removed the last of his clothes.

"Fucking hell, I can't wait to taste you." Tristan leaned forward to nuzzle Maddox's erection.

"No," Maddox barked as he pushed Tristan onto his back on the bed and then leaned over him until their cocks were pressed together.

Tristan murmured incoherently at the contact as he lifted his hips for more friction.

"No baby. Don't move. Your pleasure is mine to control." Maddox rolled his hips and grinned.

"Oh fuck," Tristan stared up into Maddox's lust filled eyes and saw them flare with heat as he said, "Yes sir."

Before he could say another word, his pants and socks had been removed and Maddox was manhandling him farther onto the bed. He gasped as he felt him pressed tight against him, skin to skin for the first time.

"I can't promise I'll be gentle. I want you too much, so tell me if I need to stop."

"Maddox," Tristan whispered as he leaned up and licked his neck, "I'm no wilting flower. Fuck me. I need you."

Maddox cursed before diving down and sealing their lips together as they dueled for control. Tristan wrapped his hands in Maddox's hair and pulled as he wrapped his leg around Maddox's hip.

He whimpered as Maddox pulled back enough to trail kisses down his neck and chest until he sucked on Tristan's nipple. He'd never realized how sensitive he was there as his back arched and he cried out Maddox's name.

Maddox bit down and looked up at Tristan with a smirk, "So needy."

"Shut up and fuck me." Tristan pleaded.

Maddox tapped Tristan's hip. "Turn over and get up on your hands and knees."

Tristan grinned as he did as he was told. He was so turned on already he could feel his cock dripping with precum and they'd barely touched.

"So fucking beautiful," Maddox said lustfully as

he ran his hands over Tristan's ass and back. "I can't wait to taste you."

Tristan shivered as he felt Maddox's hands grab handfuls of his cheeks and then pulled them apart as he blew a hot breath against his hole. A string of nonsensical sounds fell from his lips.

"You're so fucking cute." Maddox laughed.

Tristan grunted as he felt Maddox's body heat shift away before it was back. The click of the lube bottle opening was the only warning he got before the cold liquid hit him, and he gasped at the shock.

CHAPTER
Six

MADDOX HAD to fight to keep from laughing at Tristan as he jumped and growled, "A warning would have been nice."

"Ah, was that too much for you, baby?" Maddox murmured as he tapped at Tristan's hole. "Are you sure you're ready for this? I don't want to hurt you."

Tristan glared at him over his shoulder. "I'm not a fucking virgin. Fuck me already, you ass."

"Fuck your ass, you're damn right I'm going too," Maddox said as he slapped Tristan on his right cheek. "Don't be a pushy bottom."

"Stop teasing me and I wouldn't have to be."

Maddox poured more lube on his fingers and ran them up Tristan's crack and pushed against his tight ring of muscle. "Let me in, baby."

"Fucking hell," Tristan grumbled as he spread his legs wider.

"That's it, love. You're so tight, I can't wait to feel you wrapped around my cock."

He didn't waste any time before inserting a second and third finger and slowly pumping in and out as Tristan began to shudder and whimper. "You're so fucking hot, riding my hand like that."

"Stop talking and start fucking me." Tristan demanded in a growly lust filled voice.

Maddox smirked as he pulled out, lubed up his cock and lined it up with Tristan and pressed inside. "Holy fucking shit, you're so tight. Stop clenching and let me in, damn it."

"Dude, you're fucking huge. Give me a minute to adjust. It's been a bit since I've done this."

"It's just the head. If you can't take it, we can stop." Maddox laughed as he felt Tristan reach back and slap at him. "I'm kidding babe. I'm not stopping. Just tell me when you're ready."

Maddox let his head fall backwards as he counted to fifty and back down to distract himself.

"Okay, keep going. It feels so good."

"Fuck," Maddox groaned as he felt the tension in Tristan relax enough he slid in another inch. "So tight, you're killing me."

He slowly pulled out and pushed back in over and over until he was finally fully seated against Tristan.

"Fuuuccckkk."

Maddox grinned, "That's it, love. You did it. You took all of me. God, you're so hot. Your ass is squeezing the shit out of my cock. It's like a fucking vise, baby."

Tristan chuckled as he clenched his cheeks, making Maddox curse.

"That's it, you're done for now," Maddox growled as pulled out and slowly sank back in over and over until Tristan was whimpering and begging for more. "That's it baby, take my cock."

Tristan let out a loud moan as his arms shook as he tried to hold himself up. Maddox leaned down and over him, mirroring his position as he whispered into his ear, "You're so fucking sexy. And the sounds coming from you are driving me crazy."

Tristan grunted and then collapsed onto his chest. "Feel... so.... good."

Maddox smiled as he sat up and grabbed Tristan's hips, "Hold on baby, I'm just getting started." He gritted out between clenched teeth as he began to piston his hips. Alternating his angle and strokes until he could feel Tristan's legs tensing as his orgasm built to a crescendo.

"I'm coming." Tristan gasped out between labored breaths.

"Yes." Maddox agreed as he leaned down and bit Tristan's shoulder. "Come for me, baby."

Lights and fireworks burst behind his closed eyes as he felt Tristan's ass milk him as he came on Maddox's cock. "Fuck me, that's so hot." Within moments he felt his balls pull up tight and he followed his boyfriend into oblivion.

He wasn't sure how much time passed before he became aware of his surroundings and moved to the side so he wasn't squishing Tristan. "You okay?"

"Yeesss." He mumbled sleepily.

Maddox laughed and slowly pulled out of Tristan, who grunted and then sank deeper into the bed. Maddox leaned over and kissed his cheek, "Let me grab a cloth to clean us up real quick."

He climbed out of bed and turned to admire the gorgeous body that was in his bed. He couldn't recall the last time he felt so content and sated after sex. All he wanted to do was climb back in and pull Tristan back into his arms.

"Maddox?"

"Sorry," Maddox called as he raced into the bathroom, wet a washcloth with warm water, and came rushing back. He quickly cleaned them both up and then dropped the towel on the floor beside the bed.

Tristan sighed, making Maddox smile as he pulled him into his arms. Maybe he could get used to this, he thought right before he fell into a peaceful sleep.

CHAPTER
Seven

TRISTAN ACCEPTED the steaming cup of coffee from Maddox with a smile. "What's this for?"

"What, I can't bring my boyfriend a present?"

"Oh, for fuck's sake," Vic grumbled from the doorway. "I can't handle all the cuteness this early. Get your asses to the table for the huddle."

"Thank you, boyfriend. That was very sweet of you." Tristan replied as he climbed to his feet and grabbed his case file and notes.

He knew he was playing with fire with the way Maddox's eyes filled with heat every time he said that word, but he couldn't help it. Plus, he wanted everyone to know that he'd laid claim and that Maddox was off the market. And as much as he teased his man the night before at dinner, he loved the idea of Maddox wooing him and proving he really was in this for real and not as a booty call.

Vic waited for everyone to get settled. "Since you two-" He pointed at Tristan and Maddox, "-only have one vic why don't you go first?"

"We don't have much as of yet. We're still waiting on the M.E.'s report, but we have a white male, forty-eight years old, found in an alley in Ybor yesterday. He'd been dead approximately fifteen hours when we came on the scene. Name is Mark Sequoia, he's married, no kids." Tristan paused and glanced at his notes. "Dr. Zanders speculated his kidneys were removed where the body was found, based on the amount of blood at the scene."

Maddox took over. "He had no record, and no known issues or people that may have wanted to hurt him. Tampa PD canvassed the area and reported there were no witnesses and nothing suspicious."

"Cole," Tristan interjected, "If you can spare a moment, we'd appreciate it if you can check for any cameras in the area that might have picked up something. Tampa PD is supposedly working on obtaining that for us, but I'd rather we get that information sooner rather than later, if possible."

Vic's office phone rang, cutting them off. "Hang

on, let me get that. With all the publicity on the attack last week, the Mayor and media are constantly contacting me."

Everyone waited patiently until he returned. He was frowning as he handed Maddox a piece of paper. "Got another body missing organs. Get your asses down there and find out if we have a pattern starting. And the answer better be no. I really don't want another high-profile case right now."

Ensley slapped the table. "Damn it. Why do they keep getting the good ones?"

Tristan's eyes widened as he looked at his boss, "Do we have a psychiatrist on staff? If not, I think we need to find one... soon."

Ensley stuck her tongue out at him playfully. "I enjoy my job. Is that such a crime?"

"As long as you enjoy catching the ones creating the bodies, and you're not the one who creates them yourself." Tristan winked as he climbed to his feet and gathered his papers.

Maddox grabbed his keys off the desk. "We had a lot of rain overnight. Grab some booties to put over your shoes in case you get dirty. You will not be tracking mud into Scarlet."

Tristan rolled his eyes and followed his partner outside.

Maddox punched the address in the GPS. "It's only fifteen minutes away."

They rode in silence until the ringing of Tristan's phone disrupted the quiet. He frowned as he read the caller ID. He hesitated long enough that the call went to voicemail.

"Everything okay?" Maddox glanced over at him.

"Um... yeah, I'm sure it is." Tristan bit his lip as he continued to stare at his phone like it was going to come to life and attack him. "That was my mom's facility. I wasn't expecting a call..." He shrugged. "I guess I should stop worrying and see what they said, huh."

He pressed the voicemail button on his app and waited as it loaded to hit play. "Hi, this is Nicole, one of the nurses assigned to your mom. She had a fall this morning, and we just wanted to keep you informed. She's okay, just some slight bruising. If you have any questions, please feel free to give us a call back at any time."

"Does she fall a lot?" Maddox asked as Tristan stared out the passenger window.

"No, not really. I think this is maybe the second call I've gotten since she's been in there. So twice in like five years, I guess."

"Do you want to go see her when we get off?"

Tristan debated for a moment before nodding. "Yeah, I think I would. I'm overdue by a couple of days and I don't like that. Even if she doesn't know, I do. You don't have to come with me if you don't want to. I'd understand."

"What kind of boyfriend would I be if I didn't come? Now, what kind of flowers does your mom like? Even though you didn't bring anything when you met my mom or dad, I don't blame you, but I'd still like to bring something. Even if she won't remember, it may still make her happy to see them." Maddox teased.

Tristan laughed as he shook his head, "Fuck off. We barely tolerated each other when I met your mom. And if I remember correctly, you didn't even want me at that lunch. Your dad was a total surprise and hell, I'm lucky I remembered my name around him, to be honest. But as for my mom, she loves daisies. My father used to give them to her before he passed."

"Daisies it is. We'll forget about your lack of gentlemanly manners regarding my parents. No one blames you. You used to be a human, after all." He winked at him.

Tristan grinned as he rolled his eyes. "Thank you, I needed that laugh right then."

Maddox pulled the car over next to a taped off area. "All right, let's see what we have."

They flashed their badges to the cop and made their way below the pier. "Fuck, it's Bruce."

A thin man with fiery red hair nodded at them and waited next to the body. "Nice of you to join us before high tide comes in."

"See... an ass," Maddox mumbled. "Bruce, long time no see. How's the wife and kids?"

"Almost as well as your mom is doing." Bruce shot back.

Tristan laughed, "Dude, I take it you've never met his mother then? Marta is ... special."

"Like short bus special?"

"Well shit, you really want your ass kicked, don't you?" Tristan shook his head and turned to Maddox. "I see what you mean."

"I'm two years from retirement. What the hell do I care if I offend you guys?" Bruce shrugged. "Anyway, we're short on time as the tide will be in soon and it'll wash away what limited evidence is here. Local cops knew our vic well as she was a pain in the ass who always cut the fisherman's lines. She's a mermaid. Her lungs are missing." He paused and shrugged. "What else do you need to know?"

"Well known to the cops means she probably

had quite a few enemies. This one may be a little harder." Maddox chewed his lip as he studied her. "Then again, I don't see any other wounds, just like our guy yesterday, just missing organs, so not likely someone who was out to get her."

Tristan nodded, "Any witnesses? Who reported the body?"

Bruce frowned. "It's all in my report. Can you new agents not read or something?" He shook his head and motioned for the body bag. "If you've seen enough, we're going to bag her and take her in."

"Well, I'd say it's been a pleasure, but well, it hasn't," Maddox growled out as he stomped back across the sand toward the car.

"Why is it we keep getting the calls about these cases after the forensic team is already out there and done their thing? I feel like we're being given the information late. The pictures of the scene are great, but it's nice to get a look for ourselves, you know. I get it here in this instance. You can't fight mother nature after all."

Maddox nodded, "I get what you're saying, but yesterday's case they called us in from being off. It wasn't supposed to be our case, so yeah, we were late."

Tristan shrugged and nodded. "Yeah, I guess so.

Just wish we would have had more time today, you know. I feel like we're shafting the victims. Logically, I know that the water is coming in and washing everything away, so they did what they had to." He paused and blew out a breath. "Ignore me. I'm just grumpy, I guess."

"Well, look at it this way. That is the least amount of time I've ever had to spend with Bruce. Let's get back to the office and pull his reports. We can also check in with Sabrina on our guy from yesterday."

"Why did we have to come out here anyway, if we'd only get five minutes with the scene?" Tristan grumbled as he stopped beside Scarlet. "Um... I have sand on my shoes..."

Maddox got in and cracked the passenger window. "Guess you're walking then, or catching a ride with Bruce." He started the car and drove forward a few feet.

"You're never getting laid again if you move any farther," Tristan yelled with laughter.

Scarlet's engine revved as Maddox threw the car in reverse and backed up. He reached across and opened the passenger door. "Take your shoes off and put them in a bag in the trunk, then get your ass in here."

Tristan giggled as he moved to the opened truck

and removed his shoes. Never in his life had he dated anyone who made him laugh and joke like Maddox did. Even when they were at a crime scene. Maybe what Maddox had said was true. When you found your mate, everything just seemed better.

CHAPTER
Eight

MADDOX PLOPPED down in his chair right as Vic raced into their office. "So, is there a pattern?"

"We only had a minute to look at the body, but it did look like she had no wounds other than her lungs missing."

"That's a pretty big fucking wound." Vic huffed as he leaned against the doorjamb.

"Fucking Bruce was the tech and told us to look the reports up ourselves so we literally have no other info for you." Maddox rubbed his hands down his face. He already knew this was going to be a nightmare of a case.

"Well, follow up with me as soon as you have any updates." Vic tossed over his shoulder as he left.

"Should we call Sabrina first before *diving* into this vic? Get what I did there?"

"No, I didn't." Tristan grinned as he pushed some buttons on his computer keyboard. "It's a good thing you're cute sometimes."

"I'm freaking adorable. I know." Maddox gave him a cheeky smile before hitting the speaker button on the phone and dialing Sabrina.

On the fourth ring, she finally answered. "This is Sabrina Zanders."

"Hey there, it's Maddox and Tristan. We wanted to check in on our guy from yesterday and see if you're done with the autopsy?"

They waited a second as they heard typing from her end. "Okay, Mr. Sequoia did, in fact, have his kidneys removed. No other organs were taken and the only other injury was a needle mark on his neck. I sent everything off to toxicology. You are definitely looking for someone that has medical knowledge or has done this before. The incisions were clean, and it looks like care was taken when removing the kidneys. Hang on."

They waited while they heard Sabrina talking to someone before coming back on. "Your mermaid body just arrived, so we'll try to process her quickly. I don't think any of us want to find a third body."

"Thanks, Sabrina, you're the best." Maddox ended the call and blew out a breath. "I'd like to say looking for someone with medical knowledge narrows it down, but honestly, that's still millions of people."

He logged into his computer and pulled up Bruce's report.

"There isn't much to go on in his notes. Evidence seems to be minimal, because of the location or the tech...." Tristan shrugged helplessly. "We've got shit to go on right now, and this isn't helping. I know the team is overwhelmed with their case, but do you think we can get Cole to do a deep dive into their backgrounds? In the meantime, I guess we should interview the families and see what they have to say."

"We should probably pull any police reports and interview anyone that has filed a complaint against her. I have a feeling that's going to be a long list, so I'll see if Vic has some junior agents we can borrow."

Tristan sighed. "Are we doing the notification?"

Maddox nodded. "We're leads on the case, so we should. It's the worst part of the job in my opinion but I know we have to do it. Give me a harpy hopped up on shrooms that hasn't showered in a month any day."

"Well, fuck you very much. That's an image I really didn't need or want in my head," Tristan grumbled.

"Glad to be of service." Maddox gave him a cheeky smile. "Now, let's go give Vic the update, then do the notification, and a couple of interviews. On the way home from work, we can stop and visit your mom?"

Jasmina popped her head in. "Maddox, the package you requested is in the fridge."

He took out his wallet and gave her forty dollars. "You're the best. We're going to be on the road for a couple of hours. Think they'll be okay in the car?"

"Yeah, keep the windows cracked. It's cool enough that you should be fine."

"What exactly are you keeping locked in the car that we have to worry about the heat and getting air?" Tristan questioned apprehensively.

"You talk about Ensley, but you sound damned paranoid. Jasmina's sister owns a flower shop, so I had her get daisies for your mom. It's February. They'll be fine for a couple of hours while we make our rounds."

Tristan nodded as he licked his lips. "I totally forgot you asked about them. That was pretty awesome of you to do that."

Maddox walked over and kissed his cheek. "That's because I'm a freaking awesome boyfriend."

"No, an awesome boyfriend would have given me a real kiss," Tristan called out as he left their office and headed to Vic's.

Maddox couldn't wait to get him home. He'd show him what a real kiss felt like.

"Boss," Tristan greeted as he knocked on his door. "We're heading out to do notification on next of kin and then interview some of the family from yesterday's victim."

"If it's alright with you, we'll just go home at the end of the day instead of coming back here?" Maddox asked while cradling the vase of flowers from Jasmina.

Vic raised one eyebrow. "You trying for brownie points or something? Since when do you ask me permission for what you're going to do anyway? Just get your shit done and I won't breathe down your neck. That hasn't changed even if your relationship status has."

"Geez, I was just trying to be a good little agent. I'll go back to my snarky ways. Later boss." He tossed over his shoulder as he turned and left.

Maddox buckled the flowers into the backseat

and padded his duffle bag against it to keep them secure.

"Um... I don't think you treated me that nicely when you took me home." Tristan gaped in bewilderment. "I should count more than flowers, man. That's a negative in the boyfriend points for you."

"Are you saying you are as delicate as a freaking daisy? And we both know it's more about not spilling any water in Scarlet. Plus, you were so drunk that first night I took you home you could have been in a spaceship and wouldn't have remembered it." He said matter-of-factly then plugged the vic's address into GPS.

Tristan shrugged, "Still... I should rate higher than your car." He grumbled softly.

Twenty minutes later, they parked in the visitor spot of the condo building.

They rode quietly to the fifth floor and knocked on 5D.

A tiny woman with pure white hair answered the door. "Yes?"

"Are you Gertrude Jacobs?" Maddox asked.

"Yes." He could see the second the fear filled her eyes.

Maddox showed her his badge. "My name is Senior Special Agent Maddox Smith, and this is my partner Special Agent Tristan James. If we could come in for a minute, we need to talk to you."

"What did Rosalyn do this time? When her work called saying she didn't show up for her shift, I called her cousin to see if he could look up if she'd been arrested again." She waved toward the couches.

Maddox sat and leaned forward. "Why would her cousin know if she was arrested?"

"He's the district attorney. He's usually the one getting her out of the messes she makes."

Maddox inwardly groaned. "Her cousin is Zach Jacobs?"

Mrs. Jacobs nodded and smiled proudly.

"We'll call him and ask him to come over." Maddox nodded to Tristan to make the call.

"Now you're scaring me. What is going on?" Terror filled her voice.

"Does Mr. Jacobs live nearby?" Maddox stalled.

"He's across town, but this time of day I'd assume he's at the courthouse, so not too far away."

Tristan walked back and sat down.

Maddox cleared his throat. "We have some bad news. Do you want to wait for your grandson to get here?"

"Just tell me."

"We're sorry to inform you, your granddaughter

Rosalyn Jacobs died early this morning and was a victim of homicide."

She stared back at them, not saying a word.

"Do you understand what I'm telling you?" Maddox hoped the woman wasn't going to have a heart attack right then and there.

"I..." her jaw opened and closed several times. "Yes. I understand. Where did it happen?"

"She was found by the pier near the Port of Tampa." Maddox hedged.

"It was one of the fishermen, wasn't it? She was always getting them so riled up." The tears poured from the older woman's eyes.

"We're doing everything we can to get you the information you need."

The front door slammed open. "Grandma, what happened? Are you okay?" Zach Jacobs knelt in front of his grandmother and grabbed her hand.

"It's Rosalyn. These agents said she was murdered." She launched herself into his arms and sobbed.

Maddox and Tristan stayed quiet, letting them have a few minutes.

Their phones vibrated at the same time.

Tristan got up. "I'll let Vic in."

When Zach noticed Vic, he kissed the top of his

grandmother's head. "Let me talk to them. Stay here."

Vic held out his hand. "Mr. Jacobs, I'm ASAC Victor Judge with P.I.S. and these are agents Smith and James. They are overseeing your cousin's case."

He shook hands with each of them, then crossed his arms. "So, give it to me straight. What happened? What do you know?"

Vic nodded to Maddox to take over.

"Rosalyn was found this morning under the pier near the Port of Tampa. We are still waiting for the autopsy to come back."

"Okay, but you saw her, right? What do you think happened?" Zach demanded.

Maddox glanced at Vic, who nodded.

He leaned close to keep the conversation private. "She appears to be the victim of organ theft." It sounded dumb, but it was better than saying her lungs were cut out.

"I'm sorry. Did you say organ theft?" he asked incredulously.

"Yes sir. It appeared her lungs had been removed." Just saying it made Maddox shudder. What a terrible way to die.

"Her lungs?" Zach repeated in shock. "Do you think it was because she was a mermaid? Those fishermen hated her and always wanted her out of the waters there."

"It's too early in the investigation to draw any conclusions." Maddox felt helpless in the face of the man's anger.

"I want constant updates, and make sure everything you turn up is clean. Whoever did this, I want put away with no questions or fuck ups."

Vic nodded as he placed his arm around the DA's shoulders and steered him back toward his grandmother. "You need to focus on your family right now. Mrs. Jacob needs you. We can talk later, I promise."

As if missing organs wasn't enough, now they're going to have a DA breathing down their neck. This case had better not get any worse.

CHAPTER
Nine

TRISTAN TRAILED behind Maddox as they headed back to Scarlet, lost in his thoughts. No matter how many times he took part in a notification, it never got easier. He was just happy that this time he didn't cry. His anger at the injustice of it all burned too bright.

"Do you think she'll be okay?" Tristan nodded his head back towards the house. "Mrs. Jacob I mean. It can't be easy to outlive your grandchildren, let alone in such a horrific way."

"Zach is a good guy. He'll make sure she's taken care of. I think Rosalyn was her primary caregiver, so everything is going to change for them now."

As he reached for the handle on Scarlet's passenger door, he paused to glance in the back seat.

"Looks like they survived, and your precious car is still safe as well."

"Mock me all you want, but your mom is going to love them." He stuck his tongue out at Tristan and climbed into the driver's seat.

Tristan shrugged. She probably would, but she wouldn't know who gave them to her or even who Tristan was. Even on her good days, the lucidity was short and far between. He loved seeing her, but hated that she wasn't the woman he remembered. She'd have loved Maddox simply because he made Tristan happy, but she'd also love that he had a protective streak a mile wide... even if he tried to hide it behind his gruff, macho exterior.

"My mom isn't what you're going to expect. She's gotten frail and forgets what year it is. She can be mean when she gets upset, so don't take it personally. Her brain is messing with her and causing personality changes." Tristan explained after a few minutes of driving. "I just want you to know that. You should hear some of the stories I have of us growing up. You wouldn't believe it's the woman wasting away in there."

Maddox reached over and grabbed his hand. "You don't have to prepare me for anything. I'm in this with you and in our line of work. We have seen people in every condition. It's not going to scare me away. We'll spend some time with her and when you feel like it, we'll stay up for hours while you tell me all the great stories you have of her."

Tristan smiled softly and then turned to stare out the window at the passing scenery. Before he was ready, they were pulling into the facility his mother lived in. He smiled when he saw the new flowers they'd planted were blooming. It made the place look cheery and loved. He took a deep breath as he tried to make himself open the door. Finally, after a minute, he nodded to himself and climbed from the car.

"Tristan, it's good to see you." The receptionist greeted him as he walked into the lobby. "She's in her room right now. We just finished group OT, and she went back to watch some television."

"Thank you, Anne," Tristan murmured as he kept walking. Now that he was here, he felt the need to see his mom and reassure himself she was okay. He paused outside the door and glanced over his shoulder at Maddox before he knocked.

"Mom, it's me, Tristan." He called as he pushed the door open and entered. "I've brought a friend with me to meet you."

"Tristan, is that you?"

"Yeah mom, it's me." Tristan replied calmly as he moved to sit in a chair beside her recliner.

"Isn't it a bit early for school to be out? And didn't I ask you to let me know ahead of time when you're bringing a friend home with you?"

Tristan sighed and shook his head, "Yeah, momma you did. I'm sorry, I was just excited for you to meet my boyfriend."

Maddox stepped forward and offered the daisies. "Hello Mrs. James. It's nice to meet you."

She cocked her head and studied him before smiling and taking the flowers. "Those are my favorite. Call me Cora, and it's lovely to meet you." She winked and turned to Tristan. "You snagged yourself a good looking one. Nice job."

"Momma," Tristan scolded playfully.

Cora smiled and leaned back in her chair with a sigh as her attention wandered back to the television. Tristan studied his mother's face as she watched the show. For a few minutes, he'd had his mom back, and it'd almost felt like old times, but from past experience, he knew she'd already slipped away again.

Suddenly she turned and looked at him, "Tristan, when did you get here, and who's your friend?"

Tristan smiled sadly, "Hey momma, this is Maddox."

Cora frowned as she shifted in her chair. "This isn't a good day for guests. I've got a lot to do and you need to get ready for dinner. Your dad should be home soon, too."

Before he could reply, there was a knock on the door and one of the nurses stuck their head in. "Sorry to intrude on your visit. It's time for dinner. Cora, are you too sore to eat with everyone, or should I have a tray brought in here tonight?"

"Go away and stop stealing my gnomes. I've told you I'd report you if I caught you doing it again." Cora snapped.

Tristan gaped at his mom in shock as she screamed at the nurse. He'd known the personality shifts were a symptom of the disease, but this was the first time he'd actually witnessed one.

"Momma." Tristan scolded gently. "What are you talking about? What gnomes?"

"Are you the police here to investigate the theft?" Cora demanded as she looked between him and Maddox. "It's about time you did your job and arrested this harlot."

Tristan sighed and closed his eyes as he tried to

figure out how best to handle this situation without making things worse.

"Ms. James, we'll do our best to look into this and get everything resolved as quickly as possible." Maddox turned to the nurse and gestured to the hallway. "Can I speak with you for a moment, please?"

The nurse nodded and stepped back out of the room with a sad smile. Tristan stood and followed them out of the room. He wasn't sure if he'd been oblivious all this time or if this behavior was a sign things were getting worse.

"I'm sorry." The nurse said as soon as the door to Cora's room was closed. "I'm Rachel and I know we haven't been introduced yet, so I wanted to rectify that."

"Why are you apologizing? I feel like that should be my job. My mother is the one who attacked you."

Rachel shrugged. "You don't need to apologize either. I know she doesn't mean what she says. I don't take it personally. It's par for the course when you work with these patients. How are you holding up after seeing that, though?"

Tristan blew out a breath. "I really don't know. Logically I knew this would happen, but to actually see it... well, yeah, that was harder than I thought it would be. She's changed so much from the mother I knew and I'd reconciled myself to that. But tonight, that was …" Tristan trailed off and shrugged.

"I know." Rachel patted his arm in sympathy. "If it helps at all, normally she is the epitome of sweet and kind. Everyone loves her here."

Tristan smiled, "That sounds more like the mom I know."

They talked for a few more minutes before finally Rachel said her goodbyes so she could go get Cora's dinner tray. Tristan debated for a moment if he should go back in or just call it a night. Rachel had assured him she was good for the night and not to worry, but that was impossible.

"You need a minute?" Maddox asked softly as he stood next to Tristan.

"No, let's go. There's no reason to stick around tonight. She'll be asleep shortly, anyway." Tristan made his way through the home, glancing through the open doors as he went, taking in the sights and sounds of the residents interacting.

"Let's go home, babe."

Tristan nodded, "Yeah, I need food and my bed."

CHAPTER

MADDOX LOGGED INTO HIS COMPUTER, praying today would be a good day. The M.E. 's reports would be in with all kinds of leads. They'd solve the case, and go home and celebrate in each other's arms.

It was a fantasy, he knew that. Nothing was ever that easy and with how weird these cases were already, it was definitely going to get worse before it was over.

Tristan walked in and yawned loudly. "Cole said he sent us the background info on Mr. Sequoia and will have Ms. Jacob's info this afternoon."

"Damn, that was fast. I figured at least a couple of days with everything they have going on with their case."

"Word has already spread that the DA is involved. I guess Cole didn't want to be the reason we were delayed. Hopefully, he got some sleep last night."

Maddox printed out pictures of both victims and taped them to their whiteboard wall. He listed their names, ages, occupations, and approximate time of death. After reading through Sabrina's report, he wrote under the werewolf's column a note that the cause of death was exsanguination and kidneys were removed.

Tristan held up a piece of paper. "I got the list of family and friends we need to interview and the address for Mr. Sequoia's work. We could talk to the family and send rookies to talk to the rest. I don't expect anything of importance to come from them, but we need to cover our bases."

"You do realize you are technically a rookie, right?"

"But my kick ass boyfriend and partner is a Senior Special Agent. That gives me perks."

He couldn't help teasing Tristan. He was so easy to work up. "And what perks am I getting in return for saving you from grunt work?"

Tristan spun around and smacked his ass. "Right

here, baby. That's all you need. At least that's what you said last night."

"Vic, you better call HR. Someone is being inappropriate. I'm just not sure which one of them to report." Raell stood in the door, smiling at them.

Tristan froze as he felt his face burn in embarrassment. He dropped his head and shook it, "This is totally your fault, Maddox. You've corrupted me."

Maddox faked indignation. "I'm sorry. Who was slapping who's ass? I was minding my business, studying our victim wall, and you attacked me. I don't see how any of this is my fault."

Tristan gaped in shock, "O.M.G. you did not just say that. You are the master of inappropriate. Who do you think I learned it from?"

Maddox turned to Raell. "You were standing right there. Was I not the innocent victim here, minding my own business?"

Raell bit her lip and shook her head, "Nope, not gonna get in the middle of this lover's tiff. Let's leave it at you both have now been 'inappropriate' at work and leave me out of it."

"Traitor," Tristan grumbled as he moved to sit back in his chair. "I'll remember whose side you were on when you're on this side of the equation."

Raell's jaw dropped. "I didn't pick a side. I'm literally claiming I am Switzerland."

"If you are done harassing both Raell and me, can we get on the road?" Maddox smiled sweetly at Tristan.

"You're just asking to sleep on the couch tonight, aren't you?" Tristan pouted as he stood up and grabbed his things.

Maddox paused and leaned close so only Tristan could hear him. "Are you sure you want to threaten me? Can you actually handle not having me for a night?"

"Who's the sex fiend of the two of us again? I seem to remember I wasn't the one with a different partner every night and besides, I know how to use my hand and pleasure myself with thoughts of you."

"Ewww. You know we can all hear you guys no matter how quiet you are, right?" Sheppard yelled from the pod area.

"Not all of us have your superior hearing." Cole interjected. "What did they say?"

Tristan cringed, "Can we go, please, before I die of embarrassment? I swear I'm never going to get used to working with supernaturals and their enhanced abilities."

Maddox parked Scarlet on the street outside of the victim's apartment complex. "Tell me what you know before we get inside."

Tristan pulled out his phone and began to recite, "Mark Sequoia and his wife Heather moved into the neighborhood five years ago. No kids, background for Mark came back clean. Basically, a model citizen. He's a ... um Waste Management Professional, been with the same company for the last fifteen years. There's nothing that stands out on the preliminary checks we did. There is a note that she was inconsolable when notified. They did a bare bones interview, but weren't able to get much because of her emotional state."

"Awesome. This should be fun." Handling grieving victims' families was always so draining.

They knocked and waited. Maddox was about to knock again when a woman finally answered. "Yes?"

Maddox and Tristan held their badges out. "Hello, ma'am. Were with the Paranormal Investigative Services unit handling Mr. Sequoia's case. Are you Heather Sequoia?"

"No. That's my sister. She's laying down but I'll try to get her up. Come in." She led them through the house. There were no lights or TVs on. The curtains were all drawn, keeping the house in shadows of grief.

"You can sit there-" she pointed to the couch. "-let me get her."

"The air smells stale in here." Tristan whispered as he took in the room.

"I doubt she's been out of bed since they told her. The sister looks like she's barely holding it together." It was always fascinating to see the ripple effect death had on people.

The woman returned with a lady who looked just like her. They stood and waited for her to sit down.

"Ma'am, I'm Senior Special Agent Maddox Smith and this is Special Agent Tristan James. We're working on your husband's case. We're very sorry for your loss."

"Do you have any news? Do you know who did it or why?" She asked softly as fresh tears tracked down her cheeks.

"I promise you we're doing everything in our power to find out those answers. Would you be able to answer some questions for us?" He waited for her to nod. "Did your husband mention being followed or anyone watching him in the week leading up to his death?"

"Not to me, he didn't." She turned to her sister. "You talked to him the night before, right? Did he say anything to you?"

Maddox turned to the sister. "Can I get your name for our records?"

"Shirley Brown."

"Thank you. You spoke with Mr. Sequoia the night before his death?"

"Yes, I did. He'd called me to get my opinion on a surprise he was working on for Heather for their anniversary."

Heather broke down sobbing.

Shirley rubbed her back. "It's okay. We'll get through this together." She looked back at Maddox and Tristan. "My husband passed away five years ago. Heather and Mark have been helping me ever since."

"We're sorry for your loss. When you spoke to him that morning, did he sound off at all to you, or did he ever mention being followed?"

She shook her head. "No. He was excited about the surprise. He never mentioned anything out of the ordinary."

Maddox nodded as Tristan took notes. "Your husband was a waste management professional?"

The two women laughed through their tears. "He hated that politically correct language. He was a garbage man, he made a good living doing it and loved the people he worked with. He was not ashamed of his job and was proud to set people straight about it."

Maddox laughed along with him. "It sounds like he was a good man."

Heather nodded, then turned serious. "They told me someone took his kidneys. It's so horrific sounding. Why on earth would someone do that?"

"That's what we're trying to find out." Maddox assured her. "Did your husband have any enemies, or was there anyone giving him issues?"

"He never said anything. People seemed to like him, well... except for the guy across the hall. They had a feud going on for the last year or so because Mr. Jenkins plays loud music all hours of the night."

Maddox nodded. "I can understand how frustrating that must have been. Did he have any medical issues?"

"No. Healthy as a horse, as humans say. Nothing could keep my Mark down."

Maddox pulled his card out of his wallet. "I think

that's all we need for now. If you think of anything else, don't hesitate to reach out to us. We'll be in touch."

She shook their hands weakly and let Shirley lead them out.

"Thank you for going easy on her. They were high school sweethearts. She's been side by side with him for thirty years and now he's just gone. She didn't even get to say goodbye." As she finished, she hiccuped.

"We're doing everything we can to find the person responsible."

She nodded as she closed the door behind them.

"Well, that wasn't helpful at all. Not that I expected it to be. I really think these victims are being randomly chosen." Maddox drummed his fingers on the steering wheel as he thought about it.

"Well, not too random. Whoever did it would have to know that his kidneys and the mermaid's lungs were in good shape to be taken, right? Assuming it's the same person or persons behind both attacks, of course. Unless they were used in some black magic ritual or something and in that case, it wouldn't matter, I guess."

Maddox blew out a deep breath. "This case is

awesome, and I hope you hear the sarcasm dripping from every word."

"So basically we have no leads and nothing concrete to go on. Is it time for a drink now?"

"While it is five o'clock somewhere, we've got a few more interviews to do before we can clock out for the day. I want to talk to his... what do you call them... truck partners? I want to see if the guy or girl noticed anything out of the ordinary."

Tristan shrugged, "Sure, why not? I don't expect anything to come of it, but we need to make sure all our T's are crossed, otherwise Vic will be all over our asses. And no offense to the boss man, but there's only one person I want anywhere near mine and it isn't him."

"Would that be the guy you had the hot date with last night?"

Before Tristan could respond, their phones vibrated. Tristan checked his phone. "Oh nice, Cole sent us the info on Ms. Jacobs. Speaking of Cole, I know he's like the tech genius hacker of the group, and you said Raell is an expert at interrogation. Does everyone on the team have a special skill and what kind of supernatural are they?"

"Cole is the cutest koala shifter you've ever seen. You already know Raell is a siren. Reed is an

Amarok and has a photographic memory. Cross is trained in hostage interrogation and he's a Wyvern. Jasmina is a Unicorn and sharp shooter. Kiely is a behavioral analyst, empath, and a Pegasus. Sheppard is a vampire and weapons expert, and Ensley is a seer. She can see roughly one minute into the future."

"Damn. I feel inferior just being a homicide detective. You didn't say what your special skill is and I don't think bedroom skills count."

"I'm glad you think highly of my bedroom skills, but I'm also a linguist. I can speak a bunch of languages, I pick up on languages easily, and am good at recognizing dialects."

Tristan scrunched up his face. "Well, shit. I really need to step up my game if I want you guys to take me seriously as part of this team. Don't get me wrong, I'm a damn good detective. I was the youngest person to be moved into Homicide for a reason, you know."

"Aww, you'll always be special to me." Maddox patted his knee patronizingly. "You're the only one who can breathe fire, so that's something."

"You've got some explaining to do, mister." Tristan growled as he turned to glare at him. "Fire? What in the ever lovin' hell are you talking about?

How did I not know that was in my wheelhouse? What else are you holding back from me?"

Maddox wiped tears from his eyes from laughing as he smiled at Tristan, "Babe, I have no idea what your abilities are. You're the first Phoenix I've ever been around. I'm just assuming, but I promise we'll find out."

Tristan grumbled and turned back to look out the window. "Fine, I'm holding you to that."

His poor baby phoenix. He knew it wasn't nice to tease him, but really, he couldn't help himself. He liked his smile too much to stop.

CHAPTER
Eleven

"I KNOW ALL these interviews were necessary, but damned if they don't make for a long ass day." Tristan said as he climbed back into Scarlet after their last meeting of the day. He paused as he felt his phone vibrate in his pocket. He pulled it out as he dropped into the seat. "Oh, hey guess someone was listening to me. We've been invited to meet the gang at Tanner's for a drink. You up for it, old man?"

"Good with me. It's good to make an appearance once in a while for my adoring fans."

Tristan rolled his eyes, "Wow, that's a douchecanoe thing to say to your boy. You know that, right?"

Maddox smiled sheepishly. "You're right. That was an asshole thing to say. I'm sorry."

"Keep up that behavior and you'll definitely get rewarded. I'm so proud of you babe." Tristan winked as he replied to the text invite saying they were in. "They want to meet up at six. You want to go home and change or head directly there?"

"If we go home, I might not go back out. Let's just go straight there."

Tristan nodded. "Hey, should we invite Jaylen? It's been a bit since we've heard from him and I'd like to check in and make sure he's still good and there's still no kickback from helping us."

"He'd probably like that. Our next liaison meeting isn't until Monday."

Not like those meetings gave them any time to actually catch up or anything. There was always too much information to discuss and not enough time to do it in. He sent Jaylen a text and then put the phone in the cup holder. As they made the drive to the bar, he thought back to the day's events and went over them in his head once again. Sometimes when he had a minute to sit back and review like this, things would stand out that he hadn't consciously caught the first time. Not that he expected any great revelations, since nothing of importance had arisen in any of the interviews.

Before long, they were pulling into Tanner's

where he could see a few cars already parked. He really had to wonder how this place stayed open. He'd never been there when it was busy, not that he minded too much. Froggy, the bartender, was one of a kind and he loved the relaxed atmosphere.

Maddox waved to Jasmina as she got out of her car. "You guys had a rough day?"

She gave him a droll look. "We've been on a manhunt for eleven days straight. The humans are pissed, so they're coming down hard on us for not closing this yet."

Tristan giggled, "Wait, you did something straight?"

She flicked him off, then held the door open for them.

"Batten down the hatches. Trouble just walked in." Froggy yelled from behind the bar.

Maddox shook his head at him. "It hasn't been that long since we were here."

"What does that have to do with anything? If you came in here and raised hell yesterday, he'd be justified in saying it tonight. So time is relative in this instance." Tristan replied with a laugh.

"Time is relative? Okay, Einstein." Maddox put his arm around Tristan's shoulders. "Froggy, check out my boyfriend. He's so smart, isn't he?"

Froggy's jaw dropped. "Did you just use the B word? I never thought we'd see the day. I'm going to lose so much business now."

Maddox took a page from Jasmina and flicked Froggy off before heading over to join the group.

Tristan shrugged and stepped up to the bar. "Don't worry, some of the team are single. I'm sure that will help bring in some entertainment, right?"

Froggy cocked one eyebrow. "So, what's the plan tonight? Shitfaced drunk or comfortably buzzed? Need to know what to serve you and when to cut your lightweight ass off."

"I'm not a lightweight. I'm just not used to paranormal drinks. They're a league of their own. But we are technically off tomorrow, so let's play it by ear for now."

Froggy nodded, "Okay, want me to surprise you with some drinks then?"

"Um…" Tristan cringed. "I'm not sure how to answer that. Last time I let you make me a drink, it ended up with me passed out in his car."

"Which turned into you dating, so I think that's a point for me."

Tristan threw his head back in laughter. "Touché, you bastard." He shook his head as he walked over to his friends and called out a greeting.

He paused as he realized he did think of them as his friends. It was amazing how much his life had changed in the last few weeks. Now he couldn't imagine not having this group of guys and ladies at his back.

Cole threw back a shot and slammed the glass on the table. "I need about ten more of those if you expect me to work again tomorrow."

"If I wasn't already married, I'm pretty sure I'd be single now. My wife is ready to kill me." Reed agreed from where he sat on a stool.

Tristan cocked his head. "Where does she think you are right now?"

"Here." Reed gestured to the front door. "I expect her to walk in any minute. I invited her to save the peace later when I get home."

"I, for one, am glad I'm single. No one owns my time but me." Raell's declaration sounded a bit forced. "What about you Kiely, didn't you just start exclusively dating some guy a couple of weeks ago?"

Kiely shrugged. "Yeah, but he's cool. He's a pilot, so he's gone a lot, too."

Ensley scrunched her face. "Aren't you worried he'll have a girl in every port, so to speak?"

"Ha!" Sheppard laughed. "Kiely would cut his balls off if he tried anything like that. Who would be dumb enough to cheat on a federal agent? They know we have black sites, don't they?"

Cross huffed out a laugh as he nudged Sheppard's shoulder with his own. "Dude, there are civilians here. Don't let our secrets out like that."

"Hey, isn't that Jaylen on the tv?" Cole pointed to the screen behind the bar. "It looks like the humans are having a press conference and our boy is hiding in the back."

Jasmina grunted, "I bet it's about us and the fact we haven't brought the assholes to justice that destroyed downtown. Like we haven't been working our asses off to do that. With little to no help from them, I might add."

"Hey, now that's not fair. Jaylen has been doing what he can to help us. But his hands are tied right now. Give the kid a break." Cross argued as he grabbed one of the drinks Froggy had just carried over.

Ensley waved her hand at them. "What about you guys? You have two people missing organs now. How's the investigation going? If there is a third body, what organ do you think will be next?"

"Please don't let there be another one. We've got shit to go on and the last thing we need is more bodies piling up." Tristan griped. "Nobody knows shit about anything."

"Ohhh I know," Raell called out with a grin. "What if the next body part is a pair of eyes?"

"Eww, eyeballs are so gross." Jasmina shuddered.

Ensley gasped. "No, they aren't. And when they're gone, it's just bottomless pits left behind."

Tristan reached over and covered her hand with his. "Get help... please."

Everyone laughed at his deadpan delivery until, one by one, they all grew quiet as a woman approached them with a tentative smile. "Hey guys, am I intruding?"

"Who is she?" Tristan leaned over and whispered to Maddox. "Is she a badge bunny or something?"

Maddox bit off a laugh as he shook his head, "No, that would be Reed's wife, Dena. She's nice enough, really. It's just always a bit awkward when she joins us. She doesn't quite get our humor, you know."

Tristan cocked one eyebrow as he pointed at Ensley. "Babe, I don't get her humor most of the time either."

Maddox nodded with wide eyes. "None of us do. She's one of a kind."

For the next hour, they all laughed, talked, and

mingled until suddenly Froggy caught Tristan's attention as he rushed to the front door and stopped a woman from entering.

"Holy shit, do you guys know who that is?" He called out to the group in shock.

Cross frowned as he looked at the woman. "Should we?"

"That's Sicily Bronson with ABC Action News."

"Babe," Maddox snickered, "Why would we watch human news to know who she is?"

Tristan glanced over to see Froggy look over at them and then back at the woman. "I'm going to go see what's happening. I can't imagine why she'd be here at a paranormal bar. She's one hundred percent human."

As he walked up, he could hear the woman pleading with Froggy to give her five minutes in the bar.

"What's going on? Everything okay over here?" Tristan called out as he stopped beside Froggy.

"She wants to talk to your team. She wants an update on the attack downtown last week." Froggy explained as he shifted in front of her so she couldn't get past him. "I told her this was not the place for it, but she's stubborn as hell."

Tristan smiled at him and turned to Sicily. "I'm

Agent Tristan James. What can I do for you, Ms. Bronson?"

"Tristan James..." she repeated before letting out a gasp, "You're the human turned paranormal that helped bust Captain Bouchard last month."

"And you're Sicily Bronson. I know who you are too. Now, what is it I can help you with?"

"I'm looking for information on the attack downtown. And my informant told me the team assigned to the case was here."

Tristan nodded, "Well, I can honestly say I'm not on that case, so I can't tell you anything. If you want any information, you need to go through the proper channels. ASAC Judge will issue statements through the Media Relations office or you can reach out to his office and see if they will talk to you."

She jutted out her bottom lip. "You really won't give me anything? TPD isn't giving us any information about your side of the story. I think it's fair for everyone to know everything that's going on, not just part of it."

"And I said, I'm not on the case and therefore have no information I could provide. My team has been working for the last eleven days straight. They took a few hours off to decompress and regroup. They will be back at it first thing in the morning. If you give me your card and we have something we can tell you, I promise we'll call you. In the meantime, please give them some space."

She sighed as she dug in her jacket pocket and handed him her card. "That's fair. I appreciate you being open to possibly working with me. Have a good night."

"You too." Tristan waited until she'd left the bar before turning and slapping Froggy on the back. "Dude, that was awesome. You didn't have to do that, but you can bet it won't go unnoticed. It means a lot that we have someplace we can come and not feel under a microscope. You just earned yourself some very loyal customers."

Froggy's face turned red. "It was nothing. If she runs my customers off, I have nothing, so I'm happy to run interference. Plus, I've never been in a fight before. I'm always waiting for the day I can take a swing at someone."

Tristan bit his lip to keep from laughing at the other man. "You weren't thinking of hitting a human woman, were you? A reporter at that." He laughed as they headed back to the bar. "That's a sure way to get your place noticed, though."

Froggy's eyes grew wide. "Dude, no, I was just

saying I'm ready for a fight if you guys ever need me to watch your backs while you're here."

"I know man, but it's more fun to bust your balls." Tristan winked as he headed back to the group and stopped beside Maddox. "Babe, you know Froggy well?"

Maddox shrugged. "As well as you can know a bartender you spend four nights a week with?"

"There's so much wrong with that statement." Tristan shook his head. "But what I wanted to know was which team does he bat for?"

"Honestly, I have no clue. We've never talked about it and he's friendly to every customer. I've never noticed him giving more attention to one sex over another."

"Think that's part of his job description, though. I mean, the friendlier you are, the more tips you get right." Tristan glanced over his shoulder at Froggy. "I think we need to try and bring in some people and see who flips his trigger."

"Flips his trigger? How old are you? It's cute to see you trying to play matchmaker, though. I didn't know you were into that."

"It's just that he's going out of his way to watch our backs and he's been an awesome friend. I'd love to see him happy with someone. He's always here, alone, night after night."

"I guess I should feel like shit that I've been coming here for years and never thought about hooking him up with anyone?"

Tristan laughed, "That's cause you were too busy hooking up yourself."

"Touché."

"Anyway, I got Sicily's card. Figured it might come in handy one day to have a reporter we're friendly with. Don't worry though, I didn't tell her shit, and I talked her into leaving the team alone for the night too."

"Aww, thanks, buddy." Cole called out, then took another shot.

If he didn't slow down, he was definitely not going to make it to work the next day. "Should he be cut off?" Tristan asked the room at large as he watched his teammate shoot another shot. "That's gotta be like his sixth, at least."

"Try like ninth or tenth." Reed replied as he raised his glass in a salute to his partner. "But don't worry, he's never hung over the next day. Or at least he never has been up to this point."

Maddox reached up and grabbed Tristan's hand, pulling him down into his chair. "You do realize you are mothering us, right? First handling Sicily and now the drinks? It's okay to just relax and be one of us, you know."

"It's not mothering, it's showing I care." Tristan grinned as he leaned into Maddox's side. "Besides, if he's hung over, we'll have to listen to him bitch tomorrow. I was just trying to save us all the misery."

Ensley held her hand up. "I'm sorry, but if showing you care is constantly trying to get me committed to an asylum, then please care a little less."

Tristan laughed, "Nope, you just scare the shit out of me. But I mean that with love, of course."

"I know you do, sweet cheeks." She blew him a kiss.

Tristan sighed as he looked around at everyone, laughing and having a good time. If anyone had told him a couple of months ago, this would be his life, he'd have beaten the shit out of them. But now he couldn't imagine anywhere else he'd rather be than with this group of paranormals who'd welcomed him with open arms during his darkest moment.

CHAPTER

Twelve

MADDOX WAS SHOCKED. While they'd been busy with work, his dad had finished Tallie's room. And not just painted a nice scene. The walls were 3D and textured. He wouldn't have been surprised to see an actual bird fly out of the tree he'd built in the corner of the room.

"Holy hell, do you think he'd do a mural in my room?" Tristan asked as he gaped at the changes.

"What kind would you get? Like superheroes or maybe a zoo? Do you want cute little animals painted on your walls?"

"Let me guess, you'd prefer a scene from a sex boudoir or maybe Scarlet racing down the road."

"Oh, I love that. Maybe he can paint me driving

Scarlet." Maddox was only kidding, but then again, that could be cool.

"Your love of that car is truly frightening. You do realize she isn't real. You can't marry her, right?"

"I'm sorry that you have never found anything you truly love. I feel sad for you."

Tristan grimaced, "Dude, harsh. Really harsh. I'm so telling your mother what you just said to me. You almost made me cry."

"She's my mother. She'll take my side."

They raced for the bedroom door, both shouting at the same time.

"Mom."

"Marta."

They shoved at each other to get through the door and be the first to get to the kitchen, where she was making lunch for them.

"What has gotten into the two of you?" Marta scolded as she came around the corner to see them pushing each other out of the way.

"You would not believe what he just said to me." Tristan hollered in his haste to be heard over Maddox's bellows of outrage.

"Mom, he is belittling Scarlet. Trying to say she isn't real and insinuating my love for her is wrong."

"And he said that he felt sorry for me cause I've

STITCHED UNDER FIRE

never truly loved before. What does that say about him? He's dating me."

Tallie gasped. "That sounds an awful lot like you are saying you're in love with him."

Maddox elbowed him. "Aww shucks. It's okay, you can love me. I get it."

Tristan gaped at her, "What? No, I didn't say anything like that. Where did you get that? I was giving him shit about his unnatural obsession with an inanimate object."

Marta threw up her hands and turned her back on them. "Children, you are still children. Now wash your hands and come eat."

Tristan stuck his tongue out at Tallie and Maddox. "She just didn't want to hurt your feelings and agree with me. But we all know I was right."

"Oh, really." Maddox smiled, then shouted. "Oooh, mom, Tristan stuck his tongue out at you after you turned around."

"Tallie, cover your ears." Tristan exclaimed as he turned to Maddox with his hands on his hips. "You are in so much trouble right now. You just wait till we get home. My ass is closed to you, babe."

"Oh, my god. You guys are so gross." Tallie shuddered.

"You were supposed to cover your ears. Next

time, listen to me when I tell you that." Tristan giggled as he scooted down the hall away from the outraged Sprite.

Maddox washed his hands in the bathroom. When he looked at himself in the mirror, he had to do a double take. He actually looked happy. Younger even. Damn love making him think all these mushy things.

Maddox froze. Did he just think about love? When the hell did that happen?

"Stop hogging the bathroom. The rest of us have to wash up too." Tristan called as he banged on the door. "Tallie is trying to get in next, but I was in line first."

Maddox opened the door and stepped close to Tristan, giving Tallie a side eye. "I'll hold him still. You run in."

The girl's laughter rang down the hall as Tallie darted past them and slammed the door behind her.

"You Judas." Tristan smiled, "But I can't complain about having you pressed up against me, though."

"The door isn't soundproof, and you didn't tell me to cover my ears!" Tallie's muffled complaint came from the bathroom.

Marta popped her head around the corner.

"Geez. Would all of you hurry up? I didn't spend all this time making this food for it to get cold."

Tristan grinned, "Sorry Marta, we're done fooling around now. I promise."

Maddox slapped Tristan's ass as he passed him. He went to the kitchen table and grabbed one of the chairs and hid it in the pantry. He pulled out the short folding chair and put it in its place.

Tallie paused when she got to the table. "What happened to the other chair?"

Maddox smiled proudly. "I guess it broke. Last one to the table has to use the little chair."

Tallie gave him a wicked grin and got in her seat.

They waited patiently for Tristan. He barely broke stride when he walked in and saw the smaller chair. He glanced at Marta, then stared Maddox down as he sank into the seat. The table came up to his chest.

"You look so adorable." Tallie snickered.

"It's a good thing, cause this damn chair has no cushion and my ass hurts." He closed his eyes and grimaced as he realized how that sounded. "I swear that's not what you think at all."

Marta quirked her eyebrow at him. "Let's not discuss anyone's ass at the table." Maddox bit his lip to keep from laughing at Tristan. He knew he was going to get hell from him later, but he was having too much fun to stop. "Instead, why don't we talk about work? I saw something about bodies turning up with missing organs?"

Tallie cringed. "And that is okay to talk about while we're eating?"

Marta shrugged. "Sorry, dear. He's been telling me stories about work for so long I don't even bat an eye anymore at this stuff. We can talk about something else."

Tallie shook her head. "No, it's okay. I want to know about the missing organs, too."

"Actually, that's our case. We'd gotten the call about the first body when we were with you guys the other day. First one was a werewolf shifter whose kidneys were taken, and the second was a mermaid whose lungs were taken."

"That's just weird." Tallie gagged as she tried to eat her lunch. "How can you talk about that stuff so calmly?"

"It's part of our job, kid. You kind of get used to it I guess." Tristan replied with a shrug.

Marta sighed, "Those poor families. I can't even imagine what they're going through."

Tristan perked up. "Oh, I know something we can talk about." He grinned as he stared at Maddox.

"Marta, where's Silas today? I heard he spends a lot of time here, so I was surprised he didn't join us for lunch."

Maddox scowled at him.

"Yeah, when he's over, they disappear for long periods." Tallie mock whispered to Tristan.

Marta gasped. "I thought that was just between us girls."

Maddox stared daggers at Tallie. They knew how he felt about all this, and they still brought it up. Tristan was getting his payback sooner than expected.

"Excuse me," Tristan said as he pulled his phone out and frowned at the message on the screen. "Maddox, we've got to go. We've got another one."

"Oh dear, how horrible." Marta stood and rushed to a drawer. "Let me pack some of this food for you guys to eat on the way or after."

"Thanks, mom. I'm sorry we always rush out and can't stay and help clean up." Maddox kissed her cheek, then waited for the Tupperware she was filling.

She deserved a better son than him. He had to do better. She'd always been there for him and he took it for granted.

Maddox shuddered. Damn love. It was making him so sentimental.

Maddox pulled Scarlet into the parking garage. "Text says the body is on the roof of the attached building."

Tristan nodded. "Odd place to find a body."

"Maybe for humans, but babe, we're paranormals now. There is no odd. Where did we go to work on your flying?"

"The roof, you're right. I forgot about that."

They made their way into the building, took the elevator to the top floor, and then followed the signs to the roof access.

"If you could sign in on the log sheet before proceeding to the scene." The young agent called out as he held out a clipboard.

"Who was the first on scene?" Tristan asked as he waited his turn.

"A patrolman by the name of Vickers. He's standing by to answer questions. Dr. Zanders is in transit. Judd is up there processing the scene."

"Thank you." Tristan replied as he handed the

STITCHED UNDER FIRE

clipboard back and moved to head up the stairs with Maddox in the lead.

The human cop stood at the roof access door, looking ready to bolt. He looked fresh out of the academy. It was probably his first time in a paranormal building. "Vickers, right?"

"Yes, sir."

Maddox wasn't surprised the young man didn't shake hands with them. "You were first on scene? Walk us through it."

The kid nodded eagerly. "I knew it was a paranormal building, so I made sure dispatch notified your agency. On arrival, the person who called it in was waiting at the elevator. They told me they saw the deceased but didn't approach, as she was sure he was already dead and she knew she'd get sick."

"And do we know if he was actually gone at that point?" Tristan interjected.

"Unsure, sir. But when I went up, I checked his vitals, and he had no pulse. I was careful where I walked so I didn't disturb anything, I promise."

"You did good." Maddock assured the young officer. "Can you sit tight and let us check things out? Someone will be around to get your official statement."

They pushed the door open and stepped out into

the taped off staging area as they took in the scene. They saw Judd talking to some of the crime scene technicians and pointing out things to them. After a minute, the man turned and made his way to them.

"This is pretty fucked up." Judd greeted them. "Stick to the path and we can see the body." Judd led the way as he continued to talk. "Vic is approximately forty-five years old, male Gargoyle. He was in his shifted form, and his wings have been removed."

"His wings?" Tristan repeated in shock. "Aren't they like made of stone or something like that?"

Maddox and Judd laughed at his dismayed look, "Contrary to human beliefs, Gargoyle are not, they just look like they are. It's actually a very thick hide that is damn near impossible to get through." Judd explained as they came to a stop a few feet from the body.

"How did they take his wings, then?" Maddox asked as he leaned forward to get a better look.

"That is going to be a question for Sabrina. But as you can observe, they struggled to remove them. The guy's back looks like it's been hacked at, over and over, with something that wasn't quite sharp enough." Judd pointed to a small laceration.

Maddox frowned. "What can you tell us about the vic?"

"Once Dr. Zander arrives, we can give you more information. But his clothes and personal effects, which he left folded in a pile, have been bagged. The ID matches the victim. He works at an accounting office on the second floor."

Maddox stood. "Okay, we'll check it out. Have someone find us when Sabrina arrives or if you find anything we need to know."

He couldn't stop looking at the vic's back. The previous body's incisions had been so meticulous and only vital organs taken. Was this an unrelated murder? He had been thinking black market but now that a non-vital organ was taken, did that change his theory?

He blew out a breath and turned to Tristan. "Do you know how hard it is to catch a paranormal while shifted? And gargoyles are strong as fuck. I can't wait to see what Sabrina finds with this one."

"I'm honestly a little nervous to find out, and I for sure don't want to meet whatever it is in a dark alley alone."

"Yeah, I like my wings just where they are. Let's go talk to the witness."

They made their way down to the second floor and followed the signs to the office. They flashed their badges at the agent guarding the door to the room they'd put the woman in.

"Has anyone talked to her yet?"

"No sir. One of her co-workers brought her a coffee, but she's pretty messed up, so I doubt she's even touched it."

Maddox thanked the agent and then entered the office. The middle-aged woman looked up at them and burst into tears.

"I'm sorry. I can't seem to stop." She blubbered as she held up a soggy tissue to her eyes. "I just can't believe it, you know."

"We understand. I'm Senior Special Agent Smith and this is Special Agent James. And you are?"

"Trina, Trina Barton."

Maddox grabbed a tissue from the box on the desk and handed it to her. "I know this is hard, but can you tell us what happened?"

"Mr. Fields likes to fly here in the mornings. He jokes it saves on gas and gives him a chance to enjoy the sun rising. I was late coming in this morning because I had a doctor's appointment. When I arrived a little after ten, I noticed he wasn't in his office. At first I just thought maybe he was running an errand or something, you know. But he didn't leave me a note, and that wasn't like him. He's very meticulous about letting me know his agenda. I gave him a little bit of time and then started calling his cell and his home phone. When I didn't get an answer and nobody in the building had seen him. I went up to the roof. I don't know what I expected to find. I was just getting so worried, you know. That's when I saw him..."

Maddox felt for the woman. She was going to have nightmares for a while. Seeing a dead body was hard enough, let alone one that was murdered so brutally.

"I'm sorry to do this, but it could help us find out what happened. Can you answer a few questions for us?"

"Anything I can do, I will. He was the nicest boss, and I just can't imagine anyone wanting to hurt him like this."

Maddox smiled. "Have you worked with him for long?"

She smiled, "Twenty-three years. The day he started this office, he hired me and I've been by his side ever since."

"Did he have any family? Wife, kids?"

"No, he was all alone. His parents died when he was in college, and he never met a woman that could compare to his love of numbers. This job was his life."

Maddox couldn't imagine anyone liking numbers that much but to each his own. "Have you noticed anything out of the ordinary with Mr. Fields lately? Was he acting off, or have you received any strange mail or phone calls?"

Trina paused to think and then shook her head. "No, nothing at all. Things have been a bit hectic with it being tax season, you know."

"Yes, of course." Maddox agreed. He handed her one of his business cards. "If you think of anything else, please give us a call. Otherwise, you're free to go home for the day. We'll be in touch when you'll be allowed back into the office."

Maddox led them out of the office. "Man, these bodies just keep getting weirder. I mean, I'm glad it's not missing kids again, but still, this one is bizarre."

CHAPTER
Thirteen

TRISTAN FOLLOWED Maddox back up to the roof so they could check in with Sabrina. As they made their way to the stairway, Tristan studied the ceiling for any cameras.

"Did you notice the lack of monitoring? I've not seen a single one since we entered the building."

"Good point. After Sabrina, let's go talk to the building manager."

They made their way out onto the roof and waited for Sabrina to acknowledge them. From past experience he'd learned to never interrupt an M.E. when they were studying a body. They got pretty pissed off over it.

"Bout time you guys showed up." She called out

CASSIDY K. O'CONNOR & SHERI LYN

as she turned to face them. "You can come over. I've got a few things to discuss with you."

"Hey, we were here. We just went to see a witness to give you time to do your thing."

Sabrina smirked, "So our vic's been dead for a few hours. It's hard to determine the exact time, due to the weather and his gargoyle skin. They never make things easy. I'll know more once we get back to the lab. But I'd estimate sometime between six and eight am."

Maddox nodded. "That tracks with what his assistant told us. He usually flies to work."

"There isn't a tremendous amount of blood, which isn't surprising for this type of injury. The wings aren't linked to any major arteries, after all. But that being said, whoever did this was not prepared for the denseness of his skin when in this form. Take that as you will."

"Do you think this is the same killer, since it's slightly different from the other two?"

Sabrina frowned as she thought it over. "I'm not sure. Normally I could compare the depth of the cuts and the angles and things like that. But, it's going to be hard to tell for sure off that. If he was drugged as the last two bodies were, that could help link them.

Right now, I just don't know until we get some of the results back."

"The toxicology is back?"

"Yes, I sent them to you this morning. I put a rush on the second vic's and it came through late last night. It should be in your inbox, but spoiler alert, they were both dosed with the same medication."

"Hey, that's something. We assumed those two were the same killer. Fingers crossed this one has the same drug in his system and we don't have a second perp to find."

Tristan nodded his agreement. "Is there anything else we need to know?"

"Not at the moment. I've given Judd the go ahead to bag up the body. I'll try to get everything processed as quickly as possible. But no guarantees."

They said their goodbyes and headed back inside to locate the building manager. "Do you think they have one on site? How do we find out?" Tristan asked as he pressed the elevator button and waited.

"It's a management company. I hope it's okay, but I took the liberty of getting the information for you." The young officer from TPD interjected as he held out a piece of paper.

"Thank you. Way to think ahead." Tristan

grinned as he took the sheet. "You're gonna make a good cop, kid."

Maddox waited for the elevator door to close behind them. "You know, we should start keeping a list of humans we think we could work with. If Vic and Jaylen get a true liaison program going, we could cherry pick who we want."

Tristan dropped into his desk chair with a groan. "Three bodies, and we're not any closer to figuring anything out. This is ridiculous. There has to be something somewhere."

Maddox stared at his computer screen. "I'm going over both reports. There are no fingerprints, hairs, or DNA on the bodies to give us any leads."

"I sent Cole a request to do a deep dive into Mr. Fields' background, not that I'm expecting it to turn anything up." He turned to face their murder board. "I've never seen one with so few connecting strings. The vic's have nothing in common, almost as if they were totally random. But that doesn't make sense. Who would take a person's organs without knowing if they were viable?"

Tristan spun around in his chair, doing circles as

he continued to talk out loud. "I know I joked about ritual killings or some kind of black magic, but could it be something like that? Or the black market? But then, wouldn't we have a bunch more killings or missing body parts? I can't imagine these few cases would be enough for that... right?"

Maddox tapped his pen on his desk. "Good point. We should do a search and see if there are any other unsolved cases of bodies with missing organs."

"Should we check into the human organ transplant lists and see if anyone has suddenly fallen off the list?"

Maddox leaned back and stared at the ceiling. "I never thought about it. I guess it's true that paranormals don't need organ transplant lists, so checking the human list is a good idea."

"Is that something Cole can do, or should we have Vic go through the proper channels?" Tristan grinned at the absurdity of that comment and how much red tape it would involve.

"Between the manhunt and our background checks, I don't think we can ask anything else of Cole. I think Vic's going to have to do it the hard way."

"Shit." Tristan grumbled as he nodded. "I

assumed, but I was hoping for an easier resolution to the whole thing."

"Why don't you set up the search query for the medical cases in the database and I'll go give Vic the good news. Maybe on the way, I'll check the supply closet to see if we have some extra desk phones on standby."

Tristan barked out a laugh. He loved when Vic got so aggravated he'd fry his phone. He pulled up the search parameters for the database and filled them in with whatever he could think of without being too broad that thousands of hits came back, but not too limited that they had no hits at all. It was a fine line you had to walk.

Tristan opened the front door to their apartment and headed to the kitchen to grab a cold beer. "You want one?"

"Sure."

He grabbed two bottles out and opened them. He placed Maddox's on the counter as he studied the almost empty fridge. "Any ideas what you want to do for dinner? We're getting low on supplies."

"Is it too soon to say I think chicken wings sound good?"

"You are one sick puppy, Maddox Smith." Tristan laughed, "but now that you mention it...." Tristan grabbed a stack of takeout menus from the drawer and started flipping through them. "So we have a few options unless you have a favorite place."

"Anywhere that has buffalo chicken is good with me."

Tristan placed the order and leaned back against the counter to study Maddox. "Dinner will be here in about forty minutes they said."

"Forty minutes. It won't be my best work, but we could have some fun before it gets here." Maddox waggled his eyebrows at him.

"Pretty sure I said you were banned from this ass for your stunts this morning."

"Oh right. You did say something about your ass hurting. I'll let you and your delicate ass have time to heal."

"You can always make up for it on your knees. If you're good, you can make me come before dinner gets here, right?"

Maddox grabbed Tristan's shirt and pulled him close. "Baby, I can make you come five times in forty minutes."

"Fuck yes, I say prove it."

"You better grab a bottle of water. We need to keep you hydrated." Maddox growled as he dropped to his knees.

Tristan gaped at his boyfriend, "Wait, not that I'm not all for this, but can a guy really go that many times in forty minutes? Is it actually possible or is that a paranormal thing? If it is, then this is my lucky fucking day."

Maddox looked so fucking hot on his knees, looking up at Tristan.

"You are overthinking this and killing the mood. If we're lucky, you'll come a few times, and that is a paranormal thing. We recharge faster than a human male does."

Tristan bit his lip and whimpered as he watched Maddox nuzzle him through his pants. "That's so fucking hot."

Maddox grinned and mouthed his cock, leaving a wet spot as he undid the button and zipper of Tristan's pants. "Don't take your eyes off me, baby."

Tristan opened his eyes and nodded. He hadn't even realized he'd closed them. He watched as Maddox pulled his boxers down enough to free his cock.

Maddox leaned forward again and licked at the

precum beading on the tip. "You taste as good as I thought you would."

Tristan let out a soft oomph as he fought to keep his eyes open and on his boyfriend. "Suck me baby."

He'd barely gotten the words out before he felt liquid heat engulf his cock as Maddox took him all the way to the root. "Fucking hell." He moaned as he gripped Maddox's hair.

Maddox chuckled, sending vibrations through Tristan's body as he shuddered. "I'm not going to last if you do that."

Maddox pulled back and smirked, "Did I forget to mention my lack of gag reflex?"

Tristan nodded vigorously. "Yeah, you sure as fuck did. Holy hell in a handbag."

Maddox laughed as he licked up Tristan's length. "Hold on, baby. You're in for one hell of a ride."

He wasn't kidding, Tristan thought as he watched Maddox suck him back down his throat and then begin to bob his head up and down. Hallowing his cheeks as he went and even using teeth to lightly scrape against his shaft. He'd never had a blow job like this and he could only hope that when he had the chance to return the favor, he could do as good.

That was the last conscious thought he had

before his pleasure took over his rational thinking. All he could concentrate on was the hot, moist suction and the vibrating that was driving him closer and closer to the edge. He wasn't going to last long at this rate.

Maddox used his free hands to pull Tristan's pants and boxers down around his knees. Tristan whimpered as he felt Maddox's finger tap against his lips.

"Get them nice and wet for me." Maddox demanded.

Tristan opened his mouth and sucked both fingers into his mouth, using his tongue to make them slick and wet.

Maddox pulled his hand free and brought it down against Tristan's ass and slowly pushed past the ring of muscle. He spread his fingers and thrust them in and out until Tristan was begging. Within moments, he was shaking as he called out, "Fuck, I'm coming."

Maddox increased his suction as he moved his head even faster, making Tristan gasp and shudder. "Babe, stop. Too much."

Maddox pulled back with a sucking pop and smiled up at Tristan, "That was only round one."

The doorbell dinged, making them both jump.

"Sit tight, I'll be right back." Maddox winked as he jumped to his feet and raced out of the kitchen.

Tristan's legs wouldn't support him and he turned to lean against the counter, with his head against the cool surface.

"Guess you took me at my word." Maddox called out as he dropped the food on the counter beside his head. "Should we look into a plug so we don't have to do as much prep next time?"

Tristan laughed, "Kinky."

Maddox pulled open a drawer next to Tristan's hip and grabbed a bottle of lube.

"You put that in the kitchen?" Tristan glanced over his shoulder with a raised eyebrow. "What if your mother or Tallie had found it when they were here cooking?"

"Neither are virgins. It's on them if they are snooping in my junk drawer."

Tristan groaned as the cold liquid dribbled down him, "Why hasn't someone invented lube that's warm out of the bottle?"

Maddox slapped his left ass cheek, "If you want me to stop, I can try to warm it up for you. I didn't realize how sensitive you were."

"Fuck off."

"You've got that partly right." Maddox replied as

he rubbed his lubed cockhead against Tristan's hole.

"Shit, yes, fuck me." Tristan begged as he arched his back, giving Maddox better access.

"So fucking tight." Maddox gritted out between clenched teeth as he pushed in. "Hold on to the counter, love."

Tristan grunted as he felt Maddox pull almost all the way out before jerking back in with a growl of need. All he could do was sit there and take it as his boyfriend pounded into him over and over. Sweat dripped down his face as he felt drops fall from Maddox onto his back.

"You're so tight, you fit me like a glove." Maddox growled as he pulled Tristan up with his hand in his hair. "You're mine, baby. This all belongs to me, and I'm going to fuck you so hard, you'll walk funny for a week."

Tristan whimpered as he reached back and grabbed Maddox's hip and pulled him tighter against him. "Yes, oh god yes."

He lost all ability to talk as his eyes rolled back in his head and all he could do was take what Maddox was giving him. His orgasm came out of nowhere as he let out a scream and he painted the cabinets he was facing.

Maddox growled as he continued to fuck Tristan,

"Two down, one to go, baby."

Tristan collapsed back against the counter in front of him, as he bit his lip in ecstasy, "I thought you were joking."

"Fuck no."

Tristan wanted to protest, but he could already feel his body gearing up for a third one. He couldn't remember ever having two in such quick succession, let alone a third.

Maddox tapped Tristan's leg. "Put your leg up on the counter. Open yourself for me."

Tristan laughed as he tried to move his leg, but he was so shaky he wasn't sure he could do it.

"I've got you babe." Maddox said as he lifted Tristan up and held him against the counter so his one foot was off the ground. "Now I control your pleasure."

"Fuck," Tristan gasped as he felt Maddox's hand wrap around his aching cock and stroked it in time with his thrusts. Within minutes, he was a whimpering, begging mess.

"Come with me, baby." Maddox growled as he thrust faster, "That's it, take my cock."

Tristan threw his head back and screamed as he felt Maddox's hot cum fill him up, just as his orgasm slammed into him and knocked him unconscious.

CHAPTER
Fourteen

"WELL, if you boys are going to show up late to the meetings, at least you brought goodies to bribe us with." Vic called out as Maddox and Tristan entered the pod with a couple of large bags of pastries from Mrs. Diaz's food truck.

Maddox clapped Jaylen on the back. "Hey man, saw you on the T.V. the other night. You're really rising up through the ranks over there, aren't you?"

"I wouldn't call standing in the back while the big whigs do all the talking, moving up in the ranks. I'm just glad I still have a job, and that working with you guys hasn't seemed to hurt me too much."

Vic knocked twice on the table. "We got a lot to cover. Let's get started. Tristan and Maddox, with three bodies, you still have the lower body count, so you guys get to go first again."

Maddox flipped open his notebook. "The first two victims were taken out with the same drug. One had their kidneys removed and the other her lungs. The third body is a little different, but we think that's because of the type of paranormal he was. The gargoyle's back was cut up pretty brutally and his wings removed. The first two bodies had precision cuts but with gargoyles' skin being so tough, it's likely still the same perp. We're waiting on toxicology to come back with any drugs."

"So far," Tristan jumped in when Maddox stopped to take a breath. "There is nothing connecting any of the victims. Nothing out of the ordinary in the files, and family and friends don't report anything suspicious. Basically, we've got nothing so far."

"Sabrina did mention that we're probably looking for someone with a background in medicine or some equivalent because of the clean cuts and removal of the organs."

Vic nodded at them. "Okay, Jaylen. What have you got for us?"

"The press conference the other day was actually about one of the victims from your downtown attack. The girl that had been pinned in her car has gone missing while she was being transferred to another facility."

"Shit, are you serious?" Jasmina shook her head. "What the hell is going on with the world?"

"What are the chances one of the two perps that are on the run took her? I can't imagine they are trying to make witnesses disappear since there are just so many, but given we can't find them, I think we need to keep it open as a possibility." Ensley offered.

Vic nodded and turned to Cross. "And on that note, what do you guys have to report about the hunt for them?"

"Honestly?" Cross said as he leaned back in his chair with a sigh of frustration. "Not a goddamn thing. It's like they've fallen off the face of the earth."

"The family of Keith Granderson, the minotaur, said he is a survival expert so we think he's in Ocala National Forest but with 387,000 acres it's a needle in a haystack." Sheppard added.

Kiely jumped in. "Bryce Wilkinson's wife has found a couple of notes on her car and has had a fifteen second call from her husband saying things like he's sorry, and he didn't mean for any of this to happen. Other than that, dude is a ghost."

Vic looked back at Cross. "Should I have more

agents brought in to help search the forest?"

"Ooooh," Raell sat forward excitedly. "You should definitely bring Finneas and his team from the Orlando office. I always have a good time when he's here."

Maddox rolled his eyes. He didn't care how good of a lay the fae was. He didn't want him anywhere near their office. He shot daggers at Vic until the other man glanced at him and nodded slightly. Vic would never do that to Maddox. He knew how much he detested the other agent.

"The Miami office has reached out about sending people. We'll start there if you need them." Vic waited for Cross to respond.

"We already have a ton of people and we have a good system in place, so let's not mess with the flow just yet."

"I'll give you a few more days. If you guys haven't made any progress, I'm going to have to. The longer this takes, the angrier the humans become."

Tristan raised his hand, "I keep meaning to read all the paperwork I was given about P.I.S. when I started, but things have been pretty insane."

Vic raised an eyebrow. "Is there a question in there somewhere? And why in the hell are you raising your hand? This isn't school."

Tristan grinned, "How many offices are there and where are they?"

Maddox snorted. "Wow, Bruce was right. Agents don't like to read reports, do they?"

Tristan flicked him off as he smiled at Vic.

"We have offices in every major city in the U.S. and every country has their own version of P.I.S. as well."

"I've visited a few, and we by far have one of the best locations. Those Iowa agents have got to get bored out of their minds." Sheppard added.

"If no one else has anything, then let's get back to work. We're ankle deep in shit and need to close some cases." Vic grumbled as he rolled back his chair.

Maddox stopped him. "Any luck on access to the human organ transplant database?"

"You would think we were asking for access to state secrets or something. I think we'll have it by the end of the day."

Maddox nodded and went to their office. "I'm going to add the third vics info to the wall. You want to check the queries and see if we've had any hits?"

"Sure, let me run to the bathroom real quick and then I'll log in."

Maddox printed out the picture of the newest vic

and added it next to the others. As he finished writing up the details, Vic knocked on the door frame.

"We've got another one. I'll send the info to your phones. The body was just found, so forensics is on the way out there as well."

Maddox leaned his head back and sighed. "Why the fuck are they happening so fast? It's so unusual for a serial killer to be in a hurry. Not that I think that's what this is, but still, why the rush?"

"What's going on?" Tristan asked as he walked in with a fresh cup of coffee. "You get some bad news or something?"

"We both did. We got another body. Get your stuff. This one is still fresh." Maddox grabbed the coffee from Tristan and took a big gulp. "You might want to grab another for the road."

"What the hell ass, that was mine." Tristan grumbled as he turned to go back to the kitchen.

"That's not how relationships work. What's yours is mine and what's mine is mine." Maddox smirked.

"And if anyone ever questioned why he was perpetually single, now we know why."

Maddox maneuvered through the residential neighborhood as they made their way to the latest scene. He parked Scarlet in the first available spot he could find near the crime scene. "Nice area. Maybe that means we'll get lucky and someone had a video camera that might have caught something."

Tristan grunted, "Like we'd get that lucky at this point."

They signed in with the uniformed patrolman at the police boundary. "Who's in charge?" Maddox asked as he took in the area with a nod of approval as he saw the police tape was a good distance from the house and that the looky-loos were being kept back.

"We were waiting for you. Officer Bradley is on scene until you showed up though." The cop said as he raised the tape for them to walk under.

Maddox nodded his thanks and then headed for who he assumed was Bradley. He had that air of command that those in charge naturally exuded. "Officer Bradley?" Maddox held out his hand in greeting. "I'm Senior Special Agent Smith and this is Special Agent James."

He shook his hand and then smiled at Tristan, "It's been a while, Tristan. It's good to see you doing so well. I'm sorry for what happened to you. The bullshit aside, you were a damn good detective."

Tristan smiled, "Thanks, it did suck, but I'm starting to think that some things happen for a reason, you know. I've got a pretty damn good thing going now and I can't say I'd go back and change anything if I could."

Maddox grinned, "Aww shucks, we love you too."

Tristan rolled his eyes. "So, you were first on the scene?"

"Yeah, we got a call from one of the neighbors. She said the vic's front door was wide open, and that she hadn't left for work. Which was apparently very unusual for her." Officer Bradley pointed to an older lady sitting on her front porch with a walker next to her. "When I arrived, she informed me that the victim, a Carla Mathers, lived alone."

Maddox pulled out a notebook and took some notes as he listened to Bradley give his report.

"I approached the door and called out and after getting no response, I reported back to dispatch that I was going in to do a wellness check. The body was a few feet inside the doorway, not easily visible from the road. If you ask me, it looked as if she was leaving for work and was attacked. Her purse is on the ground beside her as if it was knocked off her shoulder and spilled. There was no doubt she was dead as there was a large incision across her stomach, so I stepped back out and called it in. She's listed as a paranormal, so you guys were called in and here we are."

"Thanks, we'll take over from here. Our forensic team should be here shortly as well as some of our agents to relieve your guys to go back to their duties."

"Sounds good. I know our sides don't always get along or work well together, as is evident with what happened to Tristan, but don't hold that against all of us. Some of us aren't bigoted assholes." He winked and turned back to Tristan. "If you ever want to grab a beer and catch up, give me a call."

Maddox waited until the cop was out of earshot before elbowing Tristan. "Asked out for a drink... should I be jealous?"

"Of him, hell no. He's happily married to his college sweetheart for over twenty-five years. He's salt of the earth and a damn good cop. He just doesn't handle the political stuff well, so he gets bypassed for promotions."

Maddox grinned as he waved to a group of Agent's who'd just arrived. "Two of you start canvassing the neighbors. Find out if anyone heard or saw anything out of the ordinary. Keep an eye out for any doorbell cameras. Forensics should be here any minute. In the meantime, watch the crowd for anything suspicious."

As they made their way up the driveway to the front door, Maddox glanced over his shoulder to see the elderly neighbor watching them. "We need to talk to her ourselves, see if she's a busybody and watches everything that happens with everyone, or is just friendly with our vic."

They stopped a few feet from the front door to make sure there was no evidence they could accidentally tread on.

"Are you fucking up my crime scene?" Judd called out with a grin.

"Would we do that?" Tristan shot back. "Look, we've even stopped back here not to touch anything. But now that you're here, we're eager to get in."

Judd rolled his eyes. "Let me take some pictures and tag anything out here before you go on the porch and then we can go inside. From what dispatch relayed, she's dead and rushing won't do a bit of good. I don't want to miss anything that can nail this asshole or put any doubts in the case when it goes to trial."

Maddox shrugged, "Sure, no problem. We were

just going to look so we could get a positive ID."

It only took a few minutes for Judd to wave them to the doorway. "Okay, just be careful where you step. There's a lot to tag and mark inside."

Tristan stopped at the frame of the front door and examined the lock. "No sign of forced entry, no scratches on the lock, and the frame is intact."

Maddox sighed, "Your friend is probably right with his guess, I'd say."

They stepped inside and paused to give their eyes a moment to adjust to the dim room. The body was a few feet away on her back. Her once pale blue scrubs were now dark with blood. The room showed no signs of a struggle, just the vic and her fallen purse to show something bad had gone down here.

Maddox pulled on a pair of gloves that Judd held out to him and then reached down and grabbed the wallet from the floor. "License confirms that the victim's name is Carla Mathers."

"Shit," Tristan grumbled as he scrolled through his phone, "She's a phoenix shifter. What the fuck?"

"Hello boys," Sabrina called out as she entered the house. "We really need to stop meeting like this."

Judd smirked as he kept taking pictures and tagging the evidence. Maddox grunted, "Bout time you showed up, what can you tell us?"

Sabrina cocked one eyebrow. "Well, from the two minutes I've been here, I'd say it's a dead body." She pushed past them and knelt down beside the body to examine it. "Did I hear you say she was a phoenix?"

Tristan nodded. "That's what her file says, anyway. I've been reading up on our kind. I thought with our regenerative powers we were like indestructible?"

Sabrina shook her head. "No one is indestructible. Hard to kill, but nothing is impossible." She hummed and shifted on her feet slightly. "She has an incision in the upper right quadrant of her abdomen. I'd say, and don't hold me to this just yet, but we'll probably find her liver has been removed. I'll know more once we get her back. It would also explain why she didn't regenerate. You can't live without your liver, so if it was removed…"

Tristan sighed, "Well, this case just keeps getting more and more fucked up. So, we're thinking she was what… knocked out and then they removed her liver and left her to die?"

"People are fucked up. You should know that by now." Sabrina mumbled as she stood up and moved to the other side of the body. "I can tell you that this incision isn't quite as precise as the early cases."

Maddox sighed, "All right, is there anything we need to know right now?"

"No, I'll send you a preliminary when I get back to the office." Sabrina replied absently. "But if it helps, based on rigor and body temp, I'd say she died roughly between... three and six this morning... maybe..."

"Sounds good. We'll go talk to the neighbor who called this in. Have a good day." Maddox waved at Judd and walked out and across the street.

The older woman was still sitting in the same spot. She was wringing her hands as she watched them approach. "She's not okay, is she? I knew it the second I saw that door open. A woman living alone would never be so careless."

"I'm Senior Special Agent Smith and this is Special Agent James." Maddox handed her his card. "Did you know Ms. Mathers well?"

"No. We waved when we saw each other and a couple of years ago I fell while checking the mail and she stayed with me until the ambulance came. I know she leaves at the same time every weekday for work, so when I got up to have my coffee and saw her car there and the door open, I just knew something was wrong. She didn't suffer, did she?"

Maddox steeled his expression. This woman

didn't need to know that someone stole an organ from her. "We can confirm she was murdered. Did you hear or see anything unusual this morning?"

She shook her head. "I don't sleep with my hearing aids in, so I wouldn't really hear anything before I get up."

"Have you seen anything out of the ordinary lately? Cars that don't belong or anything like that?"

"Not that I know of. I spend most of my day watching my programs, so I don't pay much attention to what's going on outside."

Maddox scanned the porch. "Do you have any security cameras or doorbell cameras?"

She snorted. "I have a flip phone if that tells you anything."

Maddox nodded. "If you do think of anything, you have my card."

They thanked her for her time and headed back to their car. Four bodies in six days didn't make sense. What was the rush? And why only paranormals? Things were not adding up, and they needed a break in this case before the counts got too much higher. Thank the stars for the destruction downtown, keeping the media busy and off their backs for once.

CHAPTER
Fifteen

BY THE TIME they'd grabbed some lunch and headed back to the office, it was midafternoon. Tristan opened his sandwich at his desk and moaned at the taste. "Is it bad to be this hungry after leaving a crime scene?"

"With how often we're around death? I'm sure it's the same for nurses and doctors." Maddox shrugged as he took a large bite of his Cuban sandwich.

"Yeah, I guess. Still always makes me think people are judging, though."

"Life is too short to care what other people think."

Tristan grunted and pulled up the database queries to see if there had been a hit yet. "I'm starting to think I used too broad of a search parameter. It's still freaking running. This is insane."

"Now you see why we all just use Cole."

"At least we finally got Sabrina's autopsy report on the first two victims. It's confirmed they both died of a combination of an overdose of Propofol and blood loss. Together, their blood pressure would have dropped rapidly, causing death within minutes."

Tristan tapped his fingers on the desk as he continued scanning the reports. "She confirmed the incisions were likely made by the same person, as the depth of the cuts and the angle are very similar. No DNA other than the vic's was found either. The perp is either very lucky or very good."

"Do you see anything on the third vic yet?"

"Not really. Toxicology is still pending. She hasn't gotten to the autopsy, but she did put in a preliminary report. Basically, not much more than we were told at the scene, though. She still believes it's the same perp as in the first two cases, but that's supposition at this point."

Maddox put a picture of the fourth victim on the wall. "So assuming they are all connected, in six days we've had kidneys, lungs, wings, and a liver taken. We're hunting Dr. Frankenstein."

Tristan laughed and then froze as his computer beeped. "We've got a hit." He exclaimed as he dropped his half-eaten sandwich and started jabbing at his keys on the computer. "Looks like we have a report of a salamander shifter who was knocked unconscious. It wasn't until a few days later when he showed up at the ER, that it was discovered he'd had his bone marrow harvested."

Maddox rushed to his side and looked over Tristan's shoulder. "So he's alive?"

"He is." Tristan pumped his fist in the air. "We've got our first break. We're getting closer. I can feel it."

"Let's not get too excited. It was days before the first dead body showed up and he lived, so it's not a total match."

"Every party needs a party pooper. That's why we invited you, party pooper." Tristan sing-songed.

Maddox pinched Tristan's side. "So mature."

Tristan laughed and leaned back in his chair to stare up at his partner. "You want to call him and set up a meeting and then get out of here? I could really use some naked cuddle time."

"It has to be naked? So specific."

"Well, yeah, duh spooning leads to forking, you know."

Maddox threw his head back and laughed loudly. "You are so weird."

Tristan grabbed his phone, hit the speaker button, and started dialing. "That's why you love me. Admit it."

Before Maddox could reply, Tristan heard the call connect. "Hello?"

"Hi, this is Special Agent Tristan James with the Paranormal Investigative Services. I'm calling in regards to a report you filed a few days ago. Would you be available to meet and answer some questions?"

"Ah, well yeah, I can do that. Is tomorrow okay? I'm working mid shift today and won't be available until late this evening."

"Sure, we can make that work. Can you come to our office around nine tomorrow morning or is that too early?"

"I can do that, sure."

Tristan thanked the man and ended the call. "I don't care what you say. We have a lead, baby."

"Hey, if it makes you feel better to hold out that hope for the next twenty-four hours, then by all means go for it."

"Well, I'd rather hold something else, but this will work for the moment." Tristan winked as he threw his sandwich in the garbage. "Let's run a check on this guy so we know as much as we can about him for tomorrow."

Tristan turned his chair to face the murder board. "If this guy is connected, it changes our time-line a bit."

"Right. If he was our first victim, why did the perp leave him alive and why wait three days before their next victim and then rush through several in a short span?"

"You know what I really want to know is why would the perp needs lungs, liver, wings, kidneys, and bone marrow? It seems too specific to not be for a reason, but for the life of me, I can't think of anything."

"I'm telling you, it's Dr. Frankenstein, and he's building a monster. There is no other explanation."

"And you call me weird." Tristan studied the board, lost in thought. "I'm going to assume talking to the latest victims' co-workers is probably going to be pointless, but we should do it to cover our bases, right?"

"We definitely need to find out if she had reported anything odd or if there were any unusual people asking questions. We should also call

Obinski and see if we can pick his brain about all this."

"Yeah, I didn't think about that. We are looking for someone trained, so the surgery center she worked at could be a clue."

Maddox dialed Obinski and put it on speaker.

"Hello."

"Hey doc, it's Maddox and Tristan."

"My two favorite P.I.S. agents. How's it going?"

"You've probably heard on the news about some bodies missing organs. It's our case and we have a lot of medical data to comb through. Do you mind if we stop by tomorrow and maybe talk it over with you?"

"Tomorrow is no good. I'm scheduled to do several procedures, but I can squeeze you in on Wednesday?"

"Great. We'll grab lunch and bring it to your office?"

"Sounds good to me. See you Wednesday."

Maddox hung up the call. "It was a terrible way we met him, but he's a great contact to have."

Tristan glanced at the clock and sighed, "I feel like all we do is hurry up and wait. Let's get to the surgery center before they close for the day. I'm keeping my fingers crossed we find something there."

The smell of cooking food was the first indication their apartment had been invaded. Then the laughter reached their ears.

"Is that Tallie and your mom?" Tristan asked as he dropped his keys on the small table inside the door.

"Sure sounds like it. What was that about wanting naked cuddle time?" Maddox kicked his shoes off and made his way to the kitchen.

"Mom, the key I gave you was for emergencies. Cooking lasagna is not an emergency." Maddox kissed her cheek.

"I could say that I missed my boys, or that I wanted to see how you guys were settling in over here. But the truth is, our power is out and won't be back on for a few hours. So, we thought we'd use your kitchen and you get a hot home cooked meal. It's a win-win."

"And I really just wanted to see if you two truly were in separate bedrooms. Yeah, I snooped. You guys are ridiculous." Tallie shook her head at them.

"Well, I hope you found something that embarrassed you." Tristan grumbled as he moved to the fridge and grabbed a bottle of water. "It'd serve you right."

"Um... do you remember what I was doing before Marta took me in? I don't think there is anything that could embarrass me."

Tristan grinned and moved to stand next to Maddox. "Wasn't it just last weekend when she was yelling at us for being gross? Can we put her new attitude to the test?"

"I'm a fickle teenager. What can I say?" She handed Maddox a stack of plates. "You guys set the table and we'll bring everything out."

"A bossy teenager, too." Maddox muttered as he took the dishes and did as he was told.

Marta laughed, "Well, boys, you'll be happy to know I did not snoop and I wouldn't let her tell me anything she did find. Though I do worry about you both. Separate bedrooms, really?"

Maddox glared at them. "Not that it's anyone else's business, but we've only been together a month. We wanted to have personal space, too."

Tallie grinned, "Marta, you'll be happy to know that unless Tristan makes his bed every day, which he never did when I was staying here, his bed was not slept in last night."

Maddox looked at Tristan. "Damn, I think we need to hire her at the agency."

Tristan laughed and nodded. "I think she'd give Vic a coronary within a day though. Guess it would depend on how much you want him to suffer."

"Where's Silas tonight?" Tallie asked as she shot a look at Maddox.

"I'm not sure. I could always call and see if he wants to join us?" Marta said innocently.

Maddox rolled his eyes. "You are trying to bait me, and it's not going to work. What mom does with her time is her own business. Until I think there's a problem, then it's my business too."

Tristan nodded slowly and turned to Marta. "You know you're always welcome to invite him here with you."

Marta chuckled. "Maddox, close your ears," she paused for a few seconds, "I appreciate the offer, but there is nothing going on with Silas and I relationship wise. When one of us has an itch, the other one scratches it."

"No offense, but the man has stuck around all these years and comes running the minute you call him. There is more to it than you're admitting to or you're just hiding from it. He's in love with you. That was as clear as can be."

Tears filled Marta's eyes. She bit her lip for a few seconds before sighing. "I know he cares for me. He has made that clear, but I don't think we'd fit together. The Fae wouldn't accept me, an Ogre. It's like Beauty and the Beast."

Maddox slammed his hand on the table. "Are you kidding me? The Fae would be lucky to have you among them. You're beautiful. Don't ever let anyone make you think otherwise."

"Tallie, do you hear these two?" Tristan questioned with a shake of his head. "They both fear the same thing and call the other out on it. Maybe it's time for an intervention of some sort."

"Already on it." Tallie waved Marta's phone in the air as she danced away from the table. "I'm calling Silas now."

Tristan watched the teenager run to the back of the apartment for privacy and laughed at her exuberance. This might backfire on them, but Maddox and Marta needed a wake up call and hopefully, this would do it. He met his partner's eyes and smiled sheepishly. "Sorry, not sorry."

Before anyone could reply, the girl was back. "He should be here any minute."

"What?" Marta's face lost all color.

"Are you serious?" Maddox looked ready to strangle someone.

The doorbell rang, startling them all. "I guess that's probably him," Tristan called over his shoulder as he headed to answer the door. He paused to prepare himself before opening the door. It was awkward as hell, but Silas' beauty was still a bit overwhelming to him.

"Hey," he greeted as he pulled open the door and smiled. "Come on in. Everyone is in the kitchen. I'm not sure what Tallie told you, but we need an intervention and you were the perfect person for it." He rambled as he led the way down the hall.

"Color me intrigued. I love a good intervention." Silas scanned the apartment as he followed Tristan. "I like the place. It looks very cozy."

Tristan grimaced, "We're still getting settled in and having a bit of a time meshing our styles. It'll come together when your son learns to be less stubborn."

They walked into the dining area. A place setting had appeared while Tristan was gone.

Silas nodded at Maddox, smiled at Tallie, and kissed the top of Marta's head. "Evening, everyone. It's rare there's food at an intervention. I like this much better." He grabbed the spatula and helped himself to a big serving of lasagna. "So, what can I help you with?"

"Well," Tristan glanced between Marta and Maddox, "It's come to our attention that Maddox feels neither the Fae nor the Ogres would accept him and Marta feels that she's too ugly for the Fae, and you're too pretty for the Ogres. It's the reason why she's kept you at a distance. And to top it all off, they both are pissed that the other feels that way."

The fork fell from Silas' hand and clattered loudly on the plate. It was a sight to behold, watching his face turn to utter rage. Tristan was shocked to see this side of him. He'd always come across as so happy and carefree, but this was a look that actually made him a bit nervous. "Should Tallie and I let you guys talk amongst yourselves?"

Maddox swung his head to him. "Leave and I will kill you. You started this. You'll suffer every second of this with me." He glanced at Tallie. "You too, squirt."

Silas nudged Tallie. "Can we switch seats? I want to talk to Maddox." Once they were situated, he reached out and grabbed Maddox's hand. "I've never understood why you wouldn't come to my home more. I had tried everything to give you a comfortable room, but you never wanted to stay. I love you and I accepted that this was always going to be the way our relationship was. If you came to my home, you would see I have pictures of you hung up and I keep every article that talks about your work. I am proud you are my son. Now that I know the true reason you keep me at arm's length, I won't stand for it. You are my son. You are beautiful, the Fae side and the Ogre side. I don't care what anyone else thinks and you shouldn't either. Every person at this table loves you just the way you are, and that is what is important in life. Everyone else can just go fuck themselves."

Maddox stared at Silas. His jaw tensing repeatedly was the only way to know he was actually listening.

Silas nudged Tallie again. "Switch back."

Tristan leaned close to Maddox's side in a gesture of comfort. His partner had a bomb dropped on him and he wanted him to know he wasn't alone.

Silas angled himself to face Marta. Tears were already rolling down her face. "Do you know how many times I've asked you to marry me?" She shook her head. "Three hundred and twelve. I remember every single time, and it crushed me to be denied. All I've ever wanted is to be with you. I want to wake up on Sunday morning and cuddle in bed with you and on a Tuesday night, I want to curl up on the couch and watch whatever rom-com you are currently obsessed with. Your beauty, generosity, and gentleness outshine any Fae I've ever met. If you asked me to leave the community, I would do it in a heartbeat. I don't need them. All I need is you," he glanced at Maddox. "And my son."

Tristan grabbed his napkin and wiped his eyes. He couldn't imagine a love so strong it had lasted through all that rejection and heartache. He hoped his mom had had it with his father, but he'd died when he was too young to recall. Maybe if he was lucky, he'd find he had it too...

"Holy shit," Tallie whispered. "That was beautiful."

Marta laughed through the tears. The teen's words helped break the tension. "If it's okay with you all, I'd like to talk to Silas privately for a moment out on the balcony."

Maddox gave the tiniest nod, but still hadn't spoken a word.

Tristan watched them walk away and then turned in his chair to face Maddox. "Babe... are you okay?"

"I don't know what to say. What words could possibly equal what he said to me? I have been so stupid for so long and lost so much time with him. I think part of my sleeping around habit was because of my parent's relationship. How different would my life be if mom and I hadn't been so stubborn and blind?" Maddox rested his head in his hands. "I am not built for this kind of vulnerability. You have to help me. What should I say?"

"You hug your father and tell him you're sorry and can't wait to get to know him. Then you follow through. You hang out with him and become friends. And most of all, you tell him you support him marrying your mother. They are in love and while they don't need your blessing, I bet they'd love to know they have it."

The sliding door to the balcony opened. Silas walked back to the table, looking dejected. "Well, that would be three hundred and thirteen times she has rejected me."

Marta came in laughing. "Only because that proposal was to go find someone who could marry us right this minute. I accepted number three hundred and fourteen when you gave me a more reasonable timeline."

Tristan jumped to his feet and hugged Marta. "I'm so excited for you guys. This is fantastic."

Tallie squealed and jumped up to join in on the

hug. "Best day ever. Can I plan your bachelorette party?"

"We have a lot to discuss, but let's let it sink in for a day, okay?"

Everyone froze when Maddox slowly pushed back from the table. His chair scraped against the floor. He walked toward them and stopped in front of Silas. "I am the biggest fucking idiot. You never gave me any reason to doubt you, but I did. I never gave you a chance and blamed you for leaving mom. I didn't know about the proposals or that you collected articles about me. We've lost a lot of time, but I hope we can start fresh." He held his hand out and waited for Silas to shake it. He held on and didn't let go. "No sex before marriage, got it?"

Silas' jaw dropped. He looked at Marta for help.

Maddox burst into laughter. "I'm just giving you a hard time. Seriously though, I'm glad mom finally said yes. I look forward to spending more time as a family."

Tristan blew out a breath, "Babe, I was so going to hurt you if you were serious. What in the hell, man?" He paused and turned to Tallie, "But for you, that's strictly enforced, young lady. Those legs are to remain closed and locked."

Tallie rolled her eyes at him. "Yes, dad."

Tristan shuddered, "Okay wow, that was seriously weird to hear out loud."

Maddox nodded. "Right? I always thought my first child would be a dog or a fish, not a surly teenager."

Marta laughed, "Okay, how about I reheat the food and we enjoy it as the family we are?"

Tristan ran to the kitchen calling out, "I think this calls for a celebratory glass of wine."

"For me too?" Tallie asked.

Four no's were shouted at the same time.

"Geez, so this is what a real family feels like."

Yeah, it does, Tristan thought as he brought the bottle to the table. With luck this would become a tradition. He could get used to being surrounded by these people who only wanted the best for each other.

CHAPTER
Sixteen

MADDOX RUBBED his chest as they walked toward the conference room.

"You okay?" Tristan gave him a worried look.

"Yeah, I guess I'm still a little sore from all that vulnerability last night."

Reed paused as he was walking by and glanced over his shoulder at them with a smirk. "Sex finally made you vulnerable. You're growing up before our eyes."

Maddox glared at him. "Ha ha, very funny."

Tristan laughed and pushed Reed away. "Leave him alone, you'll make him pout and then I'll have to deal with it all day."

Maddox knocked on the conference room door and then entered. "Thank you for coming in, Mr.

Abbott. I'm Senior Special Agent Smith and this is Special Agent James. We read over the report you filed but would like to hear it from you."

"Sure. Every evening I jog in Eagle Lake Park. That night I was running my normal route and felt a pinch on my neck. My body started going numb as I felt someone grab me from behind and drag me toward the trees. I blacked out and when I came to twenty minutes later, I was alone. My hips hurt a little, but I was just dragged, so assumed it was from that. When I got home, I noticed a puncture hole on the back of both hips, but I don't know anything about medical stuff. I had no clue what that could mean. I thought about reporting it, but I had no information and I wasn't even sure if anything had happened to me. The next day, a large bruise developed on my hips. The soreness had gotten worse and then the left hole started to drain. I knew something wasn't right. I went to the ER and told them what happened. I think they thought I was crazy. I was admitted overnight, given some IV antibiotics and fluids. While I was in there, they did an x-ray and found a small object in my left hip. They had to take me to surgery to get it out. It was embedded into my hipbone. Turns out it was a broken-off piece of needle. They can't confirm, but they believe someone took some of my bone marrow. Their theory was they did the left hip first, but when they broke the needle thing, they had to go to my right side. The doctor called you guys to come get a statement from me."

Maddox had never heard anything so crazy. "That had to be a lot to process. How are you feeling now?"

"I'm fine. Once the infection cleared up, life went back to normal."

"That's good to hear. The park you jog in, is that your usual spot? Do you run at the same time every day?"

"Yeah, it's near my house and I always run before bed, otherwise I have trouble sleeping."

"Did you notice anyone following you in the days leading up to the attack? Or anyone watching you?"

"No, but I usually have earbuds in and just zone out. I know that probably isn't smart, but I thought that was something only women had to worry about. Stupid male ego, right?"

"I get it. Sometimes we think we're impervious." Maddox pulled a sheet of paper out of a folder. "We'd like to get a copy of your hospital records. Would you sign this release form?"

"Sure, do you think they'll help you find out who did this?"

"There's a chance your case is linked to a couple of others we're working on. These records might help us prove that."

"Oh no, other people had their bone marrow taken too?"

"Not exactly, but we're not at liberty to say more right now. I'll give you my card so you can check in on our progress and when we have news, we'll reach out to you."

They thanked him for his time and had an agent escort him out and went back to their office. Tristan closed the notebook he'd been taking notes in and sighed. "What the hell? This is some seriously messed up shit."

Maddox stared at the victim wall. "Let's assume for a minute he is vic one. The new timeline is bone marrow taken on the thirteenth and vic left alive. Three days later, they start dying and having organs taken. Why the escalation?"

"Why do I feel like your Dr. Frankenstein reference is starting to feel way too close to the truth."

"Because nothing else makes sense."

Tristan frowned and nodded. "Fucking weird ass

cases. I never had anything like this when I was with TPD. What is the world coming to?"

"I don't think the world is getting worse. Paranormals just open up a lot of scientific advancements and physical abilities that humans don't have, so our cases would be different."

"Yeah, that's a good point." Tristan tapped his fingers on his desk, "Hey could Cole access the dark web and see if there is any talk of organs for sale or people looking to buy them?"

"He could probably spare some time for that. He'd much rather be on the computer than hiking through the forest."

Tristan woke his computer up. "I'm going to check the queries and make sure nothing else popped since yesterday."

Maddox dropped into his chair. "I'll check if Sabrina has sent any more reports." He scanned his email. "Nice. Looks like the final autopsy report is in for our third vic and toxicology for the fourth. Let's see what we got."

"Well, they may actually be fourth and fifth, right?"

"True, but let's wait to change the board until we know for sure he's a part of this." He scanned the computer screen. "It's confirmed that both the gargoyle and the phoenix had massive amounts of Propofol in their systems. Sabrina is positive the first three are connected. I assume when she finishes the autopsy on the fourth, she'll say she is also."

"I need to talk this out to make sure it's all correct in my head and I'm not forgetting anything." Tristan leaned forward and steepled his fingers together in front of his face. "We have four, possibly five victims. All missing some component of their body, in the span of one week. You know I can't wait to see what Obinski thinks about this. He must rue the day he met us."

"It goes both ways, though. It's always good to have an agent on speed dial." He looked at the stack of folders on his desk. "Since you got here, I have gotten so behind on paperwork. You are a real distraction, you know that?"

"Stop staring at me all the time and you wouldn't be so behind."

"You are the one sauntering around, shaking your ass in front of me."

"Guess I shouldn't tell you I have a session with Logan scheduled in a few minutes. So I'm going to be getting into my shorts and tank." Tristan stood and winked. "Too bad you have so much paperwork and have to stay here and get it done."

"You know, as the junior agent, you should be doing the paperwork. So I guess this is yours." He dropped the stack on Tristan's desk. "I'll spar with Logan until you're done."

He rushed out of the office before Tristan could argue.

Maddox grabbed a towel and wiped the sweat from his face. "I always forget how hard it is to spar with you. I did enjoy you wiping the mats with Tristan's face, though."

"Anyone ever tell you you're a fucking sadist." Tristan grumbled as he lay panting on one of the mats. "I can't feel my legs anymore."

Logan smiled proudly. "You're only as good as your weakest teammate. You don't want to be the weak link in your pod."

"Cole is a freaking Koala shifter. How much stronger can he be than me? Doesn't he just latch on and not let go?" Tristan laughed.

"Because you're a eucalyptus tree? But Logan is right, I saw him take down a perp once and dude was viscous. You definitely need to spar with him sometime. You'll be shook."

Tristan sat up. "So who would win between him and a honey badger?"

Logan tilted his head as he thought. "Honestly, never seen those two kinds fight. I think there is a honey badger on the second floor. I bet she'd be willing to spar with him. Would it be wrong to place bets?"

"Dude, I was just thinking of the betting potential." Tristan climbed to his feet and wobbled unsteadily.

Maddox shook his head at Tristan. "Cole is our pod mate. We can't bet against him. Have some loyalty."

"Would he have to know? We could do it on the downlow, right?"

Logan nodded his head eagerly. "We're agents. If we can't do something on the sly, we really suck at our jobs. I'll get working on setting up the weirdest cage match in history."

"What in the hell are you guys doing now?" Vic demanded as he walked in. "Do I even want to know what I just walked in on?"

Tristan gaped, "How... does he have super hearing or something? How did he know?"

"No one knows the true limits of Vic's powers. He

won't tell anyone what he is." Maddox whispered out the side of his mouth.

Vic stopped in front of Maddox and sighed heavily. "I swear this wasn't me. I had nothing to do with this. I didn't even know until ten minutes ago."

Maddox quirked an eyebrow.

The doors to the gym swung open. "Maddox, my old friend. It's been too long."

"Are you fucking kidding me?" Maddox stared daggers at Vic. "I thought you said you were pulling from Miami?"

Finneas crossed the mats. "Have you heard the good news? I'm here permanently. My transfer went through."

Maddox wanted to kill someone. He could see past that toothy, smarmy smile. "I hadn't heard. Our pod's full, so where'd they put you?"

"I'm not sure yet. I think I'm going to help with the manhunt, then get assigned somewhere." He held his hand out to Tristan. "You must be this guy's new partner. How lucky to get to learn from the ever impressive Maddox Smith himself."

Maddox snarled.

Tristan smiled and took his hand. "It's nice to meet you and you're right, he's pretty great. I've learned a lot from him. Welcome to the office. I look forward to getting to know you."

Finneas reached out and gave Logan a big hug. "And Logan, coolest bear I know. You still look as fit as ever."

Logan actually blushed. Did everyone fall for the Fae's bullshit?

"Good to see you. You're looking good yourself. I'm the Defensive Tactics trainer here so anytime you want to work out just let me know." Logan glanced at Maddox and shrugged.

"Well, why don't I take you up to the pod and let Cross catch you up on the case?" Vic held his arm out toward the door.

"Sure, sounds good. I'm excited about getting started." Finneas waved at them and followed Vic out.

"Can you believe that guy? What a poser." Maddox huffed.

Tristan raised one eyebrow. "What do you mean? He seems like a great guy. I don't get it."

Logan shook his head. "You'll never get it. None of us do. It's been like this since the academy. I think the guy is genuinely a nice dude."

"What's his specialty? You know, so I can feel

even more inadequate around you all." Tristan grinned to show he was kidding.

"He's got the highest tracking score of any agent in the academy's history." Maddox answered flatly.

"Yup, not inferior in the least." Tristan frowned. "Logan, make me feel better. I'll get some kind of powers or something so I can excel too, right?"

Logan flung one large arm over Tristan's shoulders. "Aww, you sure will, little buddy. Any day now." He ruffled Tristan's hair and took off for the locker room.

"Asshole." Tristan muttered as he followed behind the giant shifter. "I said make me feel better, not mock me."

Maddox wanted to laugh and smile with them, but he had a sour taste in his mouth. The office was his everything and now his arch nemesis would be there every day. Someone needed to be fired for letting this happen.

CHAPTER
Seventeen

"WHAT IS it with you and this food truck? It's like you're addicted to it or something. The food is great, but the line is always so long and I'm hungry." Tristan grumbled as he maneuvered to see how far from the front they were.

"Wow, hangry much? Want me to get you a Snickers bar while we wait? And to answer your question, I'm loyal to Mrs. Diaz. She lost her husband a few years ago, and this is all she has. I want to make sure she stays in business."

Tristan nodded. He got it. But that didn't matter to his stomach. He'd woken up late and hadn't had time to eat breakfast. And his partner was too anal to let anyone have food in Scarlet, so now here he was. "Why doesn't she move into a little storefront so she can hire help? She's busy enough. She'd do great, right?"

"I've talked to her about it before. She claims she likes the more personal touch with the truck. I think she's afraid to fail, and it will be easier to lose a truck than a whole restaurant."

He shrugged but didn't say anything else. His mind was already back on the reports they'd pulled together to bring to Dr. Obinski and what insight he might have for them. With luck, it would actually be something that would help, because even with the new information from the possible first victim, they weren't even close to figuring this shit out.

"Buenos Dias, boys." Mrs. Diaz waved at them when it was finally their turn. "What can I make for you today?"

"Three Cubans with rice and beans." He grabbed two twenties out of his wallet. "Throw whatever pastry you have left, too. Hangry over here, needs to eat something immediately."

She grabbed a pastelito off the tray and handed it to Tristan. "Here you go. Have this while I get your order ready."

Tristan grinned and took the sweet treat. "You're the best." He mumbled around his large mouthful. "So good."

When her back was to them, Maddox slipped the money into the tip jar. It was ridiculous the lengths they had to go to just to pay the woman. She wouldn't take money from them, so Maddox was forever finding ways to sneak the money to her.

In no time at all, she was handing over a bag of to-go containers. "Enjoy and come back soon. I feel like I haven't seen you in forever."

Tristan waved goodbye as Maddox told her they'd be back soon. "Are there any napkins in the bags? I don't want to get any crumbs or grease from my hands on Scarlet."

"You too good to use your pants?"

"Well, I could just not care and climb into your baby, but I was trying to be considerate, you ass."

"Geez, my boyfriend is so high maintenance." Maddox huffed dramatically as he dug in the bag for a napkin.

Tristan shook his head, "Yet you're the one who loves his car more than ninety-nine percent of the people in your life."

"That's their problem, isn't it? Maybe they should work to be as beautiful and dependable as my girl here." Maddox patted the roof of the car before sliding into the driver's seat.

Tristan grunted but didn't reply. It wasn't worth

bantering over and if he was honest, he kinda thought it was cute how attached he was to the damn thing. But if it came down to him or the car, he was seriously worried who Maddox would pick. He gingerly climbed into the car carefully to sit so he could hold the bag of food and not let anything get on the seat or floor mats. He really did deserve some recognition for how attentive he was to keeping Scarlet safe.

"Do we need to call ahead and let him know we're on our way or do you think he'll remember and we can just show up? I don't want to wait on him too long to eat. That pastry was amazing, but I'm still hungry."

Maddox rolled his eyes at him. "If it will make you feel better and guarantee you get to eat right away, go ahead and text that we are fifteen minutes away."

Before Maddox had finished speaking, Tristan was typing with one hand, making sure his grip on the bag didn't waver. "Done." He announced triumphantly.

His phone pinged just as they pulled into the parking lot of Shifter General. "He's in his office waiting for us." Tristan read as he climbed out of the car. "Don't forget the files we brought him. I can't carry them and the food."

"And we both know which is more important to you." Maddox shot back as he grabbed the pile of folders off the back seat.

"You know what they say... the way to a man's heart is through his stomach." Tristan winked at Maddox as he led the way into the lobby of the hospital. "Not that... I..." Tristan grimaced as he realized what he'd said and how it could have been interpreted. "What floor is he on again?"

"You've been there twice and can't remember? What kind of agent are you?" He pushed the fifth floor button and stepped back.

Tristan averted his eyes and shrugged. No way in hell would he admit he'd just blurted it out to try to cover up what he'd said. It was bad enough he could feel his cheeks burning. That was the last thing he needed for his partner to see and mock him. Maddox had enough ammunition as it was.

The elevator pinged and Tristan rushed through the door and down the hallway. He pushed open the office door and waved to the receptionist. "He said he was expecting us. Is it okay to go back?"

"Yes. Do you remember where to go?"

Tristan winced as her words echoed Maddox's from a few minutes ago. "Yup, all set. Thank you."

He was acting stupid, he knew it, but he couldn't seem to make himself stop. If he looked at Maddox, he was afraid of what he'd see on his face. It was better to get to Obinski and start the meeting so they could focus on what really mattered.

Obinski stood and held out his hand as they entered. "Gentlemen, good to see you again. I wish it was under better circumstances, though."

"You know we say that every time. One of these days, we need to hang out and relax. I think we've earned it." Tristan quipped as he set the bag down and started pulling out the boxes. "Hope you like Cubans, since we didn't ask and just got you one. Mrs. Diaz makes the best, so you'll love them." He rambled.

"I'll eat just about anything." He smiled as he took his lunch and sat back down.

Maddox set the pile of folders on the desk. "Do you mind if we talk through this while we eat? If I don't feed Tristan soon, he might go rabid."

Obinski raised his eyebrows in alarm. "Are you joking or is this something serious that we need to be aware of? With you being turned, unexpected stuff can come up..."

Tristan rolled his eyes. "He's just being an ass. I'm hungry, like really hungry because I didn't eat. There's nothing more to it than that. Don't worry, doc, if there was, you'd be the first person I'd call. I promise."

Obinski visibly relaxed. "Good, good. Now that that's settled, tell me about this fascinating case of yours."

Tristan nudged the files closer to him. "We've got four paranormals who have had body parts go missing over the span of about a week. A fifth just came to our attention yesterday. We're awaiting his medical records to see if he's connected or not. He couldn't tell us much that confirmed or denied it, but my gut says he was the first vic."

Obinski took a bite of his sandwich and nodded as he grabbed a pad of paper to take notes on. "What was taken exactly?"

"Kidneys, lungs, wings, liver and bone marrow." Maddox recited before Tristan could.

"And what type of paranormals are they all?"

"Wolf, Mermaid, Gargoyle, Phoenix, and Salamander, respectively."

Obinski stopped chewing and stared at them in shock. "A Phoenix? There's not that many of you around. That's alarming as hell. And how the hell did they all die?" He grumbled as he placed his Cuban down and opened the files. "I mean, how was the... attacker... able to subdue them enough to take their organs without their abilities kicking in and healing them before he could remove things?"

"That's what we were hoping you'd tell us." Tristan tapped one of the reports in front of Obinski. "As you can see, all four of the victims were dosed with Propofol. We know it's used as a sedative during surgeries, but we're not sure how it worked in this case. I mean, don't they have to have been given it constantly to stay under or something?"

Obinski shrugged, "It wears off quickly, so usually small amounts are given over the length of the procedure, but if given too large a dose the patient can go into what is called Acute Propofol Intoxication which can kill them. Basically, it lowers your blood pressure, which slows your heart rate down and you die."

"The toxicology reports came back on all four victims with high levels of the drug in their systems. The M.E. concluded that's what killed them. Is that why they were unable to heal themselves?"

Obinski nodded at Tristan, "Without a doubt. If everything is slowed down in your body, then that would include your healing abilities as well. It's not magic that repairs our injuries, we do that ourselves."

"We also thought the timing was odd. Once in a while, you get a random case of an organ taken, but it's usually one vic in an area and they are left alive. This is a lot of organs in one area all within a week. It's way off pattern to normal organ theft cases." Maddox added.

"What strikes me about this whole thing is that the only cases are paranormal." Obinski glanced between the two men. "Right? There are no human victims that you just didn't include..."

"We checked with the TPD and they have no reports of any, so yes, it's just these four or five cases." Tristan confirmed.

"Paranormals don't need transplants, without the introduction of the anesthetic, we'd heal from any injury or damage done to our bodies and organs. It would have to be something of a very large scale to stop the repair." Obinski leaned back in his chair as he thought about it for a minute. "They'd have to be going to a human or multiple humans. It doesn't make sense that a paranormal would need an organ from so many different types. That being said, there is no record of a human getting paranormal organs. I'm not even sure if it's possible to do it. The moral objections alone would be astronomical to most of the human population."

Maddox nodded. "Agreed. I entertained the idea of a rogue supe taking the organs to eat, but usually when that happens, it's the same organ, not a different one with each body. And they are usually ripped out. These were meticulously removed."

Tristan grimaced, "We have our boss looking to see if anyone has dropped off the transplant list without explanation, but he's running into a bit of red tape. We're looking into the black market to see if there is a sudden demand for them as well." Tristan closed the lid on the empty container and sighed. "What is really odd to me is the timeline. If the first guy is connected, his bone marrow was taken on the thirteenth, the fifteenth the kidneys, the seventeenth lungs, the nineteenth wings, and then the next day the liver. That's a total of eight days from start to finish. Why the rush? Are these random cases or were they targeted?"

Obinski raised his hands in surrender. "I don't know why the timeline, but I can tell you that if it is going to a human, then there is some equipment and supplies they would have to have on hand. For instance, anti-rejection meds, blood, and IV fluids, to name a few. The anti-rejection meds are iffy, though.

I don't know if they would work with our organs, but it's a possibility to look into at the least. You can check hospitals, vets and clinics. I don't know if it'll help, but it's a starting point."

Tristan frowned as he jotted down some notes on a piece of paper he'd swiped from Obinski's pad. "At this point, we'll take any clues or guesses you have. We're fumbling in the dark on this one." He paused and glanced at Maddox. "Do you happen to have access to a patient's records that were treated here? He signed a release for us to get his records, but it's going to take a few days before we get them."

"Technically yes," Obinski nodded, "Though we're not supposed to access patient's records that aren't ours or that we're not involved in the care of." He hesitated for a moment before he shook his mouse to wake his computer. "But if the patient signed the release, it shouldn't be an issue and the only way they'd look to see who accessed the patient's chart is if said patient had them check it."

"We don't want you to get in any trouble." Tristan interjected quickly. "We can wait."

Obinski waved his hand. "Do you have a copy of the consent?"

Tristan nodded as he grabbed one of the files

and started flipping through it. "Here, it's got all the information you should need."

"Give me a minute to log in and we'll see what I can find out." Obinski typed on the keyboard, frowned at his screen, and then typed some more. "Okay, here we go. So they did a tox screen with the blood work. They did find traces of Propofol in his system, but obviously not a lethal dose. He's a salamander shifter..." Obinski tapped his fingers on his desk and then nodded, "Okay, I can't believe I'm saying this, but did you know that salamanders can regrow body parts? What if his bone marrow was taken because of that? I can't think of another reason why they'd take that from him. Your perp would need some specialized equipment to use it so you can add that to your list."

Tristan wrote down the information as quickly as Obinski recited it.

"You're definitely looking for someone with medical knowledge. The average person wouldn't have the knowledge needed to pull any of this off. The amount of bone marrow taken wouldn't be enough on its own. He'd have to separate..." He trailed off and laughed. "The specifics don't matter. Basically, what I'm saying is whoever it is, is well trained and has access to a lot of equipment."

"I've got a question that's bugging me." Tristan said as he folded the paper and put it in his pocket. "Three of the victims lost major organs and the fourth his wings? That makes no sense to me at all. I can even see the bone marrow being important. But wings, really..."

Obinski shrugged and closed the folders. "Honestly, there are a lot of things that are weird about this case, but yeah, that is at the top of the list. I hope this helped you figure this out. If you need anything, you know where to find me."

"We appreciate you taking time from your day and we do need to plan to meet up again when work isn't involved." Maddox shook his hand before turning to leave.

Tristan said his goodbye and followed behind his partner, lost in his head. Why did it seem like they had more questions now than they had before they'd come? "I guess when we get back to the office I can start a new search for medical equipment and meds gone missing and hope something pops."

THEY FINISHED the morning pod meeting and went back to stare at the victim board. The questions were taking up more space than the facts, and that really pissed Maddox off.

Tristan glanced up from his computer. "You look like you're thinking really hard."

"I just had an unpleasant thought. I was thinking about what was said the other night about someone taking eyeballs. First of all, eyeballs are gross. Second, that's just wrong. Eyes are the windows to the soul. You can't take those from another person." Maddox shivered.

"You are so fucking weird sometimes." Tristan shook his head with a laugh.

"My weirdness is part of my charm... accept that now." He gave him a cheeky smile.

Tristan's computer beeped. "Nice. The queries are coming back already. And we have a potential breakthrough. St. Bernadette's Hospital reported missing equipment and medication."

Maddox glanced over his shoulder. "Nice. We definitely need to follow up on that. Keep searching. We're finally getting somewhere."

Commotion in the pod area had them racing over to the door. Maddox popped his head out and saw most of the team strapping on vests. "What's happening?"

Jasmina smiled excitedly. "We have a positive ID on our dragon perp. We're going to raid the warehouse."

Maddox and Tristan glanced at each other and then looked at Vic. "Need a couple of extra hands? Our reports aren't changing. We could use the change of scenery."

Finneas walked out of the equipment locker area. "What a great idea. Vic, you should definitely let them come along."

Maddox ignored the Fae and continued waiting for Vic to respond.

Vic shrugged. "Yeah, come on. If we don't get one

of them soon, the director is going to start calling for heads."

Tristan fist pumped the air, "Yes, action."

Maddox waved him to follow him. "Let's get you some tactical gear. We all know you love having P.I.S. all over you."

"I fucking hate you." Tristan fumed as he stomped out of their office toward the locker. "Stupid ass name. I swear for such intelligent people you think they'd have come up with something with a better acronym."

"Well, they were going to do the Association of Shifters and Supernaturals, but that seemed worse."

"A.S.S... Yeah, there is something seriously wrong with the powers that be. Or maybe they were trying to tell the world something with P.I.S. and ASS.."

Vic rolled his eyes at Maddox. "Would you stop making shit up? You make us sound like idiots."

Tristan spun around and gaped at Maddox, "You are such an ass. I can't believe the lies you tell with a straight face and to me, your boyfriend. That's just wrong."

Maddox walked up so he was face to face with him. "I'm sorry, honey. I promise not to do that anymore." He bit his cheek to keep from laughing.

"You suck. You just lied about lying." Tristan shook his head and turned to Vic. "What is this world coming to when you can't even trust your partner?"

Vic shrugged and walked out of the area. Maddox grabbed Tristan's elbow and pulled him against him. "Look at my eyes. You can always count on me. I will never lie to you about anything real."

"Just stupid stuff to make me look like an idiot in front of coworkers." Tristan laughed and leaned forward to kiss him. "I guess I can live with that."

"I'm trying to help you not be so gullible. It's not a good personality trait of an agent. But it's fucking adorable in a boyfriend." He kissed Tristan and stepped past him.

Tristan grunted, "Can't blame me for falling for this one. I mean, they did name the agency P.I.S. after all, so it wasn't that farfetched."

Cole popped his head in the door. "Party train is leaving with or without you. Get a move on."

The trail of agents rushed out to the parking lot and climbed into the armored vehicles.

Maddox knocked on the wall. "Don't worry. This metal is rated to withstand dragon fire."

"Like I'm going to fall for your shit again so soon."

Sheppard elbowed him. "He's serious this time. This thing could probably drive through a volcano and make it out fine."

Maddox gave Tristan a stupid smile. "Told you I wouldn't lie about serious things."

"And the truck's metal never crossed my mind as a serious thing." Tristan shook his head with a small smile.

"You'll think about it next time you are chasing an Aitvaras." Kiely winked at him.

Maddox snorted. "Really Kiely?"

"What? I haven't heard of that supe before." Tristan looked back and forth between them.

Finneas chimed in. "An Aitvaras is a fire rooster. I'm pretty sure this thing could run it over before it even did any damage."

"Sure why not." Tristan frowned. "You guys are all assholes, you know that?"

"Get serious. We're pulling up." Vic interrupted.

The trucks pulled over, and everyone filed out. "Okay, Jasmina, you go on the roof across the street. Everyone else will split into two groups. Half going in the front and the other half in the back."

Maddox felt the energy and excitement building in him. He loved a good chase.

Jasmina radioed she was set and saw no movement in any of the windows.

"Okay, get in place."

The groups split and got into position. Vic radioed Cole. "Breach on my mark... Three... two... one."

The front and back doors were rammed open at the same time. Agents flooded in and surrounded a person in the middle of the room.

A small woman was standing there with her arms up. "You aren't going to find him. He's already gone."

Vic cursed. "I'll stay with her. The rest of you clear the building."

Maddox and Tristan ran up the stairs and split off on the fourth floor. Most of the walls of the abandoned building had crumbled long ago, so there were few hiding places.

"We have his sleeping area on the fifth floor," Finneas called over the radio.

They finished clearing the floor. "Four is clear, heading up." Maddox radioed and took the stairs two at a time.

Finneas and Cole were standing over a twin mattress. They were looking through the garbage and papers scattered around.

Cole tossed an empty bottle to the side. "He was definitely staying here this whole time."

"Do you need us to finish clearing the floor?" Maddox asked.

"No, we're done. You can head down. We'll call in forensics to go through all this."

They made their way down the five flights and stopped behind Vic. The woman was handcuffed and sitting on a chair. "Did you know your husband was here the whole time?"

"Nope. I got a note with this address on my car this morning and I came here. I've never been here before."

Kiely was standing behind the woman. She shook her head at Vic.

Vic sighed. "We need you to start telling us the truth. The longer your husband is on the run, the worse this is going to be for him."

"My husband is a good man who doesn't deserve what you are going to do to him." She sneered at them.

"People are dead because of him."

"More people are alive because of him."

Vic tilted his head. "What do you mean? You never mentioned this before."

She shrugged. "I'm not saying anything else.

There's no point. Now, I didn't do anything so can you please let me go?"

"Not after saying something like that. We need to talk some more." Vic nodded at Kiely and let her lead the woman out to a waiting agency car.

Finneas and Cole joined the group. "His scent is still very strong. We must have missed him by seconds."

"Do you have any clue what she was talking about?" Tristan asked the group.

Vic shook his head. "We have no motive for why the fight even happened. Even if he was trying to do good, he helped cause millions in damage and humans died. That can't be ignored."

Maddox sighed. "This was a serious letdown. I was really looking forward to burning off some energy."

Finneas clapped his back. "I know how we can do that."

Tristan raised an eyebrow. "I sure hope it's not the way I was going to suggest."

Finneas shrugged. "Were you thinking of sparring with Logan too?"

Maddox let out a breath he didn't know he had been holding. He'd thought Finneas was suggesting something much more sexual. Thank god he wasn't.

Maddox didn't need that complication in his life. Having the Fae there now full-time was headache enough.

Tristan smirked, "That is a great way to work off some steam. And it did work the other day, even if I got my butt kicked."

Maddox hung back so he and Tristan were the last to walk out. "Screw sparring with Logan. I know exactly what you were going to suggest and I am all for it. You better be ready as soon as we're done working today."

Maddox heard Tristan moan quietly as he walked out the door. Working with your boyfriend certainly had some fun perks.

TRISTAN PUSHED OPEN the apartment door with a sigh, "God, it's been a long ass couple of days." He paused as he pulled his phone out of his pocket and scowled. "I've got to take this. It's Mom's place."

Maddox nodded and headed down the hallway as Tristan answered the call. He listened as they gave him an update on his mom's care and what the doctor had said about her fall the other day. He said yes and no at the appropriate times, but his mind was only half listening as they weren't telling him anything new.

By the time the call was over, he was ready for a shower and to relax. He headed to his room to drop off his gun when he heard the shower running in Maddox's room. Apparently, they had the same idea.

He raced into his room, locked up his weapon, and then headed back to Maddox's bathroom.

He pushed open the cracked bathroom door and let out some of the steam. "Care if I join you?" He called out above the pounding water.

"I left the door open for you, didn't I?"

Tristan smiled as he quickly undressed and then climbed in behind his boyfriend and placed a kiss on his back. "I think it's my turn for a taste."

Maddock turned to face him and cocked an eyebrow. "You think I'm going to turn that down?"

Tristan winked as he lowered himself to his knees in front of Maddox. "I have a fantasy, but I've never trusted a guy enough to try it with."

"And you're telling me this while you are on your knees?" Maddox grinned down at him.

"It's a part of the fantasy, not necessarily in the shower, but I'm flexible." Tristan shrugged as he ran his hands up Maddox's leg.

"I can honestly say I'd love to hear and fulfill any fantasy you have... well, within reason, of course. I do have some limits."

Tristan laughed, "Oh, I do too. But I promise this one is tame enough it won't push any limits."

Maddox smirked, "And what is this fantasy and if it's tame, why haven't you trusted anyone to do it?"

"I want you to fuck my mouth." Tristan glanced up at Maddox from beneath his lashes. "Wrap your hands in my hair and use me for your pleasure."

"Is that all? It will be my pleasure to fuck your mouth. Now open up and take me all the way in."

Tristan didn't waste any time doing as he was told. His mouth was watering at the thought of what was to come and he wasn't sure if he'd ever been as hard as he was right now.

Maddox rubbed his cock against Tristan's lips, "Tap my leg if you need me to stop."

Tristan stuck his tongue out and licked at the tip as he gazed up at Maddox. He might be on his knees, but he had the power right now, and that did heady things to him.

"Fuck, baby." Maddox growled as he let his head fall back as Tristan took him as deep as he could.

Tristan pulled back and licked his lips. "I'm ready."

Maddox nodded as he pushed back into Tristan's wet heat and then pulled back slowly. Savoring the moment before he began to thrust. "Relax your throat. You can take all of me. I know you can."

Tristan moaned his agreement, as he felt Maddox grip his hair tighter. He loved knowing his man was taking his pleasure from him.

"That's so good, baby." Maddox murmured. "That's right, suck me, take it all. You're such a cock whore, baby."

Tristan's eyes watered as he felt Maddox push into his throat and sit there for a moment, blocking his airway. He swallowed reflexively and felt the shudder that went through Maddox. "Fucking hell, baby."

Maddox pulled back and then back in, making Tristan grip his thighs as he held on.

"So good… yeah, baby… that's it, suck me… fuck, baby, I'm coming."

Tristan groaned as he felt Maddox's thrusts began to get more erratic.

"Tap if you don't want me to come in your mouth." Maddox paused and then groaned. "That's it baby, just like that."

Tristan relaxed as much as he could so Maddox could take his throat as his orgasm overtook him and he hunched over Tristan's back, shaking.

"Are you okay?" He asked quietly as he pulled back and let Tristan take a deep breath once again.

He sat back on his heels and smiled up at Maddox. "Fucking perfect." His voice was gravely, and it made him shiver at the sound.

"Let me take care of you."

Tristan laughed bashfully. "No need. I came when you did."

Maddox laughed and pulled Tristan up to his feet and placed a kiss on his lips. "You are so fucking perfect, baby."

"Does that mean you'll make me some tea with honey? My throat's a bit sore."

Tristan winked as he shifted behind Maddox so he was under the water and began to wash up. He was tired and sated and ready for a nap and then maybe round two. His ass was feeling a bit neglected after all.

CHAPTER
Twenty

MADDOX HANDED Tristan a cup of coffee and sat down next to him. "Today's going to be a good day, right? We have a lead to follow up on and there hasn't been a new body in four days."

"I hope that doesn't mean the perp left the area."

Maddox glared at him. "Way to dampen the excitement."

Vic slapped his notepad on the table as Jaylen walked into the pod area. "Okay. Now that everyone is here, let's get started. Maddox, Tristan, you're up."

Maddox sat forward excitedly. "After this, we're heading out. Dr. Obinski said our perp would likely need certain items, so I did a keyword search. St. Bernadette's Hospital reported missing inventory and some of our stuff is on the list. It's a long shot, but it's the best we have right now."

Vic nodded. "Good. That's a human hospital. Jaylen, would you accompany them to make the humans feel more comfortable?"

Jaylen nodded. "I was just there the other day giving an update to the father of the missing girl from the downtown attack. He's a pathologist there. Super nice guy. He lost his wife a few years ago to cancer and now this."

"Glad I didn't interview him. I can imagine how much pain he must be in." Kiely shook her head in sympathy.

"He's still working while his daughter is missing?" Shepherd asked.

Jaylen nodded. "He told me he was going insane at home, so wanted to work to keep busy."

"Keep us updated on what you find with the hospital." Vic turned to Cole. "What's the latest on the manhunt?"

"We released the wife this morning. She likely had known where he was, but she's not admitting to it. We're going to keep someone on her around the clock. We're making headway in the forest. No sign so far of our perp."

"I, for one, am really tired of the forest. If one more mosquito bites me, I'm going to lose my shit."

Maddox didn't envy them. "At least it's not summer. You guys would be dealing with heat stroke, too." Maybe they did have the better case. At least they weren't hiking through the swamp.

Maddox and Tristan let Jaylen lead the way in the hospital. It was one of the few times Maddox wore his P.I.S. jacket. Humans tended to leave them be when they saw they were agents.

Jaylen flashed his badge to the volunteers at the reception desk. "Hi. We'd like to speak with Summer Donaldson."

"I'll call and see if she's available. You can have a seat over there." The woman ignored Maddox and Tristan.

Maddox stuffed himself into a chair. "I know we're big compared to a human, but come on. You guys always have the tiniest damn chairs. I feel like I'm sitting in a chair made for a child."

As soon as he got situated, a young woman walked over to Jaylen.

"Afternoon. I'm Summer Donaldson."

Jaylen shook her hand. "I'm Jaylen Rose with Tampa PD and these are agents Smith and James with P.I.S."

She nodded to both of them. That was a nice change of pace from the usual glares and sneers.

"My office is just down the hall."

She led the trio to a small conference room she had to badge into. "We're taking this theft very seriously. We've set up a task force of sorts here. You can imagine with a hospital this big, we have a lot of security footage to comb through and people to interview."

Inside, three men and a woman were around a table working on laptops. Several screens were rolled in with pictures of people on them.

"This is so much bigger than we first reported. As we started going through all the inventory systems, we noticed a lot more missing."

She handed Jaylen a piece of paper with a list of items on it. Maddox and Tristan glanced over his shoulder. Maddox whistled, "This is basically a shopping list of everything Dr. Obinski said our perp would need."

Tristan shook his head. "Yep, anti-rejection

meds, antibiotics, IV bags, tubing, Propofol, surgical kits."

"Holy shit. Rib spreader and a bone saw?" Jaylen's jaw dropped.

Maddox shrugged. "If it's our perp, that makes sense. They'll need them to swap the lungs."

The humans all whipped their heads toward them. "Someone is swapping lungs?"

Maddox shook his head. "We have a case we're working on. We're not saying they're connected." He turned his attention back to Summer. "Do you have any suspects yet?"

Summer pointed at the televisions. "This is everyone who swiped their badges in the areas where the items were taken or that looked like they were leaving the hospital with something suspicious."

Tristan whistled. "That's a lot of suspects."

Jaylen pointed to a picture in the bottom right corner of the first screen. "That's Dr. Rogers, the dad of the missing girl. I just talked to him here two days ago."

One of the men flipped through a notebook. "He's at the top of our list to interview. He's the only person on the list who badged into every one of these areas."

Maddox gave Tristan a side eye. This was a turn of events they weren't expecting. "Is there a possibility you could do your interview today while we're here?"

Summer nodded. "We can send someone to see if he's available."

She glanced at the other woman, who got up and left.

Ten minutes and a lot of small talk later, the woman returned. "Dr. Rogers didn't show up for work yesterday or today. They've been calling him, but he hasn't answered. They were going to call about a welfare check today because they worried about him with everything that he's been dealing with."

Tristan glanced between Maddox and Jaylen. "You guys are thinking it too, right? He has to be the one who took his daughter? It's the only thing that makes sense… right?"

Jaylen nodded. "It is looking awfully suspicious. I have his home address. Should we go check on him?"

Maddox shook his head. "Can you let your detective know about the development and see if they'll send a team over? Then I'd like to set up a meeting between our teams and get synced up. I'd like to stay here and look into Dr. Rogers."

Jaylen pulled out his phone and stepped out of the room.

CHAPTER
Twenty-One

TRISTAN BIT his lip as he studied the Doctor's picture. "This is going to sound weird, but he looks so normal."

Maddox shrugged, "Don't they always?"

"True." Tristan nodded as he turned back to the room and watched the staff working. "Ma'am, do you have a breakdown of when the items were listed as stolen and from what department? Also, can we get a copy of the logs?"

Summer hesitated and then nodded. "Of course. The ventilator was discovered missing from the maintenance department on the eighteenth. The next day, we got a report of the anti-rejection and Propofol missing. Then we did a hospital wide inventory and discovered the other items. That's what led us to file the report with the police."

"And what date was that?" Tristan clarified.

"On the twentieth," Summer frowned, "Today is the first time anyone from the police department has shown any interest."

"To be honest, we're with P.I.S. so we weren't notified of this case. We stopped in because we came across it in the database and felt it might be connected to what we were working on." Tristan took the papers one of the other staff handed him. "And just to clarify, you don't have exact dates, just when things were noticed missing?"

"Yes, that's right. The ventilator had been sent down to maintenance. It can take a few days before they get to it. On the eighteenth, it was discovered missing after an extensive search."

Tristan nodded. "And do you know what date it was delivered to them?"

Summer turned and grabbed a sheet of paper from the table behind them. "The thirteenth. We can possibly give educated guesses if we base it off when the badges were used to access the areas. And that's if we go based on Dr. Roger's card swipes."

"And you said he was the only person it shows who entered all the areas?"

"Yes, and considering his position in the hospital, he really didn't have any reason to be in some of them." She paused as she glanced around the room. "I'm going to be honest with you. I'm not sure what it is you're investigating here, but based on what is missing..." She trailed off and shuddered. "There are a lot of things that could have been removed that we don't track."

"Do you know the Doctor?" Maddox questioned.

"No, the hospital is huge and I don't really get involved unless there is some reason to. We investigate the reports of questionable practices or procedures and patient care."

"I assume there is someone we can talk with that would be able to answer some questions."

"We can have his supervisor come down?"

Maddox nodded. "That would be great."

One of the guy's picked up a phone and called upstairs.

After a back and forth, he hung up. "Sheila will be down in just a minute."

Summer walked toward the door. "We'll interview her in my office. No one outside of this room knows how big this is."

Jaylen joined them as they followed her out and

across the hall. "You guys can go inside. I need to grab one more chair."

Summer came back, pushing a chair. "Sheila, hello, you can join us in here."

The woman in her late fifties went from smiling to scared the second she saw them in the room. "Am I in trouble?"

Summer shook her head. "Not at all."

"We wanted to ask some questions about one of the Doctors on staff. Can you tell us your full name and credentials for our records, please?" Tristan reassured her.

"I'm the Medical Director, Sheila Carpenter, D.O."

"How long have you worked with Dr. Rogers?"

"He joined our staff about five years ago." Dr. Carpenter folded her hands on the table and leaned forward. "But I worked with him a few times through the years when he was a Medical Examiner before he came to work here."

"I thought he was a pathologist?" Maddox asked.

"When his wife got sick with cancer, he took a leave of absence. Then when she passed away, he switched to a job with a more stable schedule so he could be there for his daughter. He did his residency and then, when he was done, we hired him as a pathologist."

Tristan and Maddox shared a look.

Jaylen pulled out a small notepad and pen. "Obviously Dr. Rogers was under a lot of stress these last couple of weeks with his daughter missing, but did you notice him acting out of character?"

Sheila glanced at Summer. "Did something happen to Brian?"

Summer cleared her throat. "I'm going to ask that you keep this confidential until we are certain we have all the details. It appears Dr. Rogers has stolen a lot of equipment and medicine from various departments over the last couple of weeks and now he has disappeared."

Jaylen jumped back in. "It looks to us like maybe he was the one who took his daughter and stole these supplies to take care of her."

Sheila shook her head vigorously. "That doesn't sound like Brian at all. He has been an exemplary employee since day one. You really think he faked his daughter's kidnapping? Every day he came in here he looked absolutely miserable waiting for word on her whereabouts."

"He stopped in or called the department for updates multiple times a day... Until two days ago."

Jaylen acknowledged. "We aren't saying he took her, but we have to be open to every possibility and go where the evidence takes us."

Summer handed her a sheet of paper. "These are all locations that Dr. Rogers has badged into over the last two weeks. We went back in his history and these are not normal areas he works in. Do you know of a work assignment or anything that would explain why he was in these locations?"

Sheila took the paper with a shaking hand and read over it. "I can't think of any reason he would have been. I'd have to check the computer to see what he's been working on to be absolutely sure though. I don't want to say that and then it turns out he had a valid reason and I have trouble believing he'd do anything like this."

"I'm already pulling up the reports now," Summer replied as she turned the monitor so they could all see it. "I don't see any cases out of the ordinary here, do you, Doctor?"

Sheila studied the cases, occasionally clicking on a report for more information before finally letting out a pained sigh and shaking her head. "There is nothing here that would require him to access those places."

"It would seem he also accessed the shifter database." Summer pointed to a couple of lines on the computer screen. "And on multiple dates during the same time frame."

Maddox leaned forward. "Can you give us the username he signed in with? We have access to the database and can see what he was looking at."

Summer grabbed a sticky note and copied down the name, then handed it to him.

One of the men from the conference room stuck his head around the door. "Summer, there are some detectives here to see you."

Maddox and Tristan stood and moved to the door as two TPD detectives stepped into the room and scowled at them. "This is our case. We'll be taking over from here. This is a human issue. We don't need you."

Maddox glared at them. "You didn't even have this lead until we found it. You should be thanking us for doing your job."

Jaylen sighed and pushed on Maddox's shoulder. "That's not going to help the situation at all. I'll call you guys later and fill you in. Please, don't make a scene that could cause trouble for me."

Tristan scoffed, "No offense, but they were assholes, even when I worked with them. There was a reason their closure rate was almost nonexistent after all."

Jaylen groaned as he shook his head at them. "Fuck my life."

Tristan winked at the scowling detectives as he pushed past them. "Later boys, we've got some real police work to do."

He almost felt bad for riling them up, but he was never one to sit back and let guys like that think they'd won. He'd make it up to Jaylen later, but for now, they had a lead to follow, and with luck, a murderer to stop before anyone else died.

Tristan stood over Maddox's shoulder as he pulled up the shifter database and entered the doctor's ID into the search fields. "Is it weird I feel like we went from nothing but dead ends to a neon sign saying guilty really quick? Not that I'm complaining or anything."

"The victims would definitely say we took way too long getting to this point. This is good police work. We worked on every lead, big or small, and finally one paid off."

"Yeah, I know you're right."

A pop-up appeared on the screen with a list of file numbers. Maddox whistled. "Geez, he looked up a lot of shifters for not having any valid reason to be in here."

"I'm counting twelve different accounts... can we look at them and see if we can figure out why those?"

Maddox clicked on the first file number. "Can you write these on the board? The first is a sixty-year-old male wolf shifter. Second is a sixteen-year-old female tiger shifter. The third is our fourth victim, Brian Fields. Four is our second victim Mark Sequoia. Five is a forty-two-year-old female gargoyle. Six is victim one, Mr. Charles Abbott. Seven is a thirty-five-year-old merman. Eight is victim three, Rosalyn Jacobs. Nine is a twenty-year-old female unicorn. Ten is victim five Carla Mathers. Eleven is... holy shit."

Maddox sat back, staring at the screen. He shook his head and sat forward again. "Twelve is-"

Tristan scowled as he turned and stared at Maddox. "What? What are you trying to hide? Who or what was number eleven?"

Maddox blew out a breath. "It's your file. He looked you up."

"Me," Tristan repeated in shock as he moved to look at the screen as if to verify for himself what

Maddox was saying. "That's my file." He confirmed softly. "Was he... the Phoenix..." He trailed off as he dropped into his seat and stared blankly.

"He likely saw you were in law enforcement and went with Carla instead."

"Yeah, cause that doesn't make me feel guilty as shit." Tristan snapped irritably. "And I feel violated. I know it's just a file, but to know some rando looked me up and then chose that woman to kill instead." He blew out a breath and closed his eyes. "I feel like I need to go to her family or friends and apologize for her being targeted instead of me."

Maddox sent the report to print and walked over to Tristan. He put a hand on each armrest and forced Tristan to look up at him. "The only person responsible for Carla's death is Brian Rogers. You didn't ask to be targeted or skipped." He kissed his forehead, then turned and grabbed the paper off the printer. "Besides, you don't know why he chose her over you. Maybe he saw your picture and thought you were too pretty to be a part of whatever he's doing." Maddox gave him a cheeky smile and ran out.

Tristan huffed out a small laugh and then sobered up as he stared at the picture of Carla on their board. "I'm sorry." He whispered quietly. He knew it wasn't his fault, but logic didn't matter right now.

Maddox walked back in. "I've got some junior agents doing welfare checks on the rest of the list. We need to make sure we don't have more victims that we just haven't found yet."

"I was just thinking we should have asked for the kid's medical records. We really don't know much about her. Do you think the team has that information? Or Jaylen, if nothing else, right?" Tristan pulled his phone from his pocket and sent a text.

> Tristan: Hey man, sorry about earlier. I'll buy you a beer to make up for it later.

> Jaylen: Damn right you will. These guys are assholes on a good day.

> Tristan: Does that mean this is a bad time to ask for a favor...

> Tristan: Maddox says he'll owe you one in exchange ;D

> Jaylen: Did he or are you just offering your boy toy up without his knowledge?

> Tristan: .... would I do that? And can you get us a copy of the daughter's medical records?

> **Jaylen:** YES you would and we all know it.

> **Jaylen:** But I have the records and can forward them over or bring them by if you want.

Tristan: We need them asap…

> **Jaylen:** Fine, give me five minutes and I'll send them to your email.

> **Jaylen:** But I want an update soon on what you've found.

Trisan put his phone down and smirked up at Maddox, "Her reports will be here shortly and all it'll cost you is one favor to Jaylen to be redeemed when he needs it."

"You just left it open-ended like that? Never agree to deals without stipulations. Do I get to have a safe word?"

"Ohhhh," Tristan bit his lip as he looked Maddox up and down, "You kinky boy, I had no idea you were into that. We can explore later if that's your thing."

Vic groaned in the doorway. "This is a place of business. Seriously, you two. Have some respect for the sanctity of this office." He glared at them before bursting into laughter. "I tried to keep a straight face, couldn't do it."

Maddox shook his head. "You had me seriously questioning your sanity there for a second."

Vic shrugged. "I question it all the time. Anyway, this morning you guys had nothing and now you may have your suspect. What the hell happened at the hospital?"

"Right now, we have a lot of circumstantial evidence pointing to Dr. Brian Rogers. He's the father of the missing girl Jaylen told us about. He works at the hospital and it's not confirmed yet, but it appears he stole a lot of medical equipment and medicine and then disappeared two days ago. We found out he'd accessed the shifter database and there were twelve names on the list. Five of them are our victims, the other six are having welfare checks done, and the last was Tristan."

"The missing teenager from the attack downtown?" Vic confirmed. "That's quite an interesting turn of events. So you think he's behind the organ thefts and it just so happens his daughter who was hurt in the attack is now missing..."

Tristan sat up suddenly. "You think he has a grudge against paranormals now?" He stopped and cocked his head in thought. "No, that's not right either.... Cause he would kill them, but not necessarily remove body parts."

"He lost his wife and possibly his daughter. He could just be fucking crazy now. Maybe he's using the organs to do sacrifices to some god to save his daughter. Who the fuck knows why these idiots think the way they do?" Maddox shook his head in disgust.

Tristan grunted as his computer beeped, alerting him that an email had come in. "I think these are her medical records." He hummed softly as he scrolled through the email. "Let me print these so you can read them, too. But from what I'm reading, she was basically crushed in the attack. They basically advised taking her off the machines and letting her go, but Dr. Rogers refused and was having her transferred to a private facility."

Vic nodded as he skimmed one of the sheets. "But it doesn't list any of the organs that we know were stolen as being damaged in the attack. This doesn't make sense."

"Or why the wings?" Tristan agreed.

Maddox tapped his pen absently on his desk while he read the report. "I think it's your turn to owe Jaylen an open-ended favor. We need TPDs' files on the disappearance. The doctor has to be with his daughter and we need to find him. Maybe there is something about the daughter that will point the way."

Tristan laughed as he picked up his phone and typed. "I'm sending the message, so I get to choose who owes who here."

Vic rolled his eyes. "Just have him come here as soon as he can and we can debrief him then. It'll be easier that way and we can all be on the same page. The rest of the team can be included, as it would seem both cases are now related, at least loosely."

"He replied, he's stuck with the detectives, but he can be here first thing in the morning with the files and the latest updates."

CHAPTER
Twenty-Two

ENERGY BUZZED THROUGH MADDOX. Any time he felt like he was close on a case, he'd get antsy and not be able to sleep. He just wanted to get to the finish line. They still had a long way to go with this one, but for the first time in almost three weeks he felt like they were on the right track.

Jaylen walked into the pod carrying a large box. "I come bearing gifts. Don't get too excited though, it's just our case files."

The box thumped heavily on the table. Thank goodness the whole team was here. With this many people, they could get through the files quickly.

Vic grabbed a file and started passing them around the table. "Can you give us a rundown?"

Jaylen nodded as he took a file. "As you know, the hospital wanted to take Quinn Rogers off life support. Brian Rogers refused and demanded she be moved to a private facility to continue her care. When the doctor showed up at the facility and discovered she'd never arrived, they called the police. The ambulance was found a few days later, burned. The ambulance had been stolen that morning from a private company and they didn't have GPS tracking on their trucks. The driver of the ambulance had a hat on and kept her face well hidden from the hospital cameras. Hospital staff said there was a male paramedic in the back, but he never came out of the truck. We confirmed they didn't work for the private company and they never had a transport scheduled with Dr. Rogers. Forensics haven't been able to find any usable evidence among all the ash and debris."

"What about traffic cameras?" Cole asked as he flipped through the file he was holding. "Were you able to track it at all?"

Jaylen shook his head. "The hospital had cameras outside their ER Bays, but once they left there... they didn't show up on any of the traffic cameras. There aren't as many in that area as you would think, though."

Tristan frowned. "So basically no way of connecting Dr. Rogers with any of it."

Vic dropped the file he'd been reading. "I'll talk to the brass over at TPD and work out a deal. We need to have a press conference again, this time with us included. We'll put out a plea for help on finding Quinn, and say we're worried about Dr. Rogers as he's gone missing as well. Someone, somewhere, has to know something."

"Do you think they'll do it?" Jaylen questioned skeptically. "Things haven't improved over there towards you guys, you know."

"Why don't we force their hand?" Everyone stopped to stare at Maddox. "Announce we're holding a joint task force with TPD at five o'clock today. That'll give us six hours to get in sync and once we announce it's happening, they can't cancel it."

Vic threw his head back and laughed. "That is going to piss them off to no end, but after all the bullshit they pull with keeping shit from us, I'm all for a little payback."

Jaylen winced. "Shit, I really am going to get fired one of these days for working with you assholes."

Maddox glanced at Tristan. "So crazy, Jaylen didn't make it into the liaison meeting today. He

wasn't here to find out we're holding a press conference later." He turned to Jaylen. "There you go, plau-
sible deniability."

Maddox stood behind the podium and held his
hand out. The TPD detective from the hospital
reached out and shook his hand. He had a smile on
his face as he muttered. "You are fucking assholes.
This was a cheap trick."

"You're just upset you got outplayed by a paranormal." Maddox smiled back.

Vic cleared his throat. "To your corners boys."

Chief Barlowe stood next to Vic at the podium.
He didn't look happy, but he acknowledged P.I.S.
had the breakthrough and would lead the
conference.

Vic cleared his throat into the microphone.
"Good afternoon. Thank you all for coming so late
on a Friday. I'm ASAC Victor Judge with Paranormal
Investigative Services and this is Chief Henry
Barlowe with Tampa Police Department. As you are
aware, TPD has been searching for Quinn Rogers,
who was taken while being transported via a private
ambulance service on February tenth. Two days

later, the ambulance was found abandoned near Roosevelt Boulevard and Ulmerton Road. We are asking anyone who may have been in the area between the tenth and twelfth to call into the TPD tip line if you saw anything that may help us. We're also very sad to report that Dr. Brian Rogers, the girl's father, has gone missing as well. He hasn't been seen for two days and we're worried about his safety. We're distributing pictures of the ambulance and of Dr. Rogers. If anyone has any information, no matter how small, please call into the tip line. We want to reunite this family safely."

Reporters shouted all at once. One voice was louder than the others. "Why is your agency involved in this? These are humans missing."

"Thank you all for coming. We're not taking any questions today."

They cleared the area quickly and went into an adjoining conference room. Vic shook the Chief's hand. "That went well. It's good to see our departments working so well together." He glanced over at Maddox, who was still having a stare down with the detective.

"Maybe we don't have those two working the tip line at the same time." Chief Barlowe mumbled.

"I got it." Tristan laughed as he walked over and

pulled Maddox to the side. "Come on, we're on phone duty for a bit."

The next few hours were mind-numbing as they took call after call with tips, suggestions, and some outright bizarre theories.

Maddox got up and stretched. "I refuse to answer another call. I'm done." He glanced around. "Jaylen, Tristan, let's go. Froggy has a beer with my name on it."

"Thank you." Tristan groaned as he stood up and followed after his partner. "I think my ass has gone numb."

Jaylen bounced up, smiling. "I don't know what you guys are talking about. I love talking to people. They are so fascinating."

Tristan stared at the other man like he had two heads. "Dude, maybe we need to get you in with a psychiatrist or something. Those people were certifiable."

Maddox shook his head at him. "What is with you and wanting to lock everyone up in a psych ward?"

"I never said that, just that they might need medication to balance out their crazy. I'm starting to wonder if it's contagious."

Jaylen shook his head with a laugh. "I'll meet you guys there."

Ten minutes of beautiful silence later, they arrived at Tanner's. "Maybe this was a bad idea. The idea of going into a noisy place right now makes my head hurt."

"Yeah, it's a Friday night too. But you know we owe Jaylen a drink and we haven't seen Froggy in a few days. We don't want him to think we've forsaken him, right?" Tristan winked. "And what if your stalker Dustin is in there? He might need some new spank bank material."

"Really, all you did was convince me even more I don't want to go inside." Maddox grumbled as he shut off Scarlet and got out. "Let's get this over with."

Tristan laughed as he climbed out of the car. "You are too easy, babe."

Jaylen walked up and laughed. "That's what's written on the bathroom stall, too."

"How do you know I didn't write it?" Maddox tossed over his shoulder as he went inside.

Froggy called out to them over the noise. "Long time no see. Grab a seat. I'll be over in a minute."

Maddox flopped into a booth and dragged himself over to give Tristan room. "Talking to people drains me. I did way too much peopling today."

"No shit." Tristan agreed with a sigh. "And where do they come up with the crap? I swear not one call had anything useful. Unless you believe the Aliens took them both away in their spaceship like two callers told me."

Maddox snorted. "The best one I got was that Disney World had taken her and sold her in a human trafficking ring and then took the dad to shut him up."

Jaylen gaped, "Mickey Mouse? What the fuck is wrong with people? Don't mess with the mouse, man."

Froggy walked up and leaned on the table. "Gentleman. You all look worse for wear. What can I get you?"

"How about three Crusty Sunburns? Make one on the easy side for the human." Tristan grinned up at Froggy.

Jaylen shrugged. "From what I hear, you may need one of the lighter ones, too. Didn't Maddox have to carry you home after one?"

Tristan glowered at the other man. "Fuck off, dude. They were strong as hell and I downed a couple of them in rapid succession."

"I'm sure Tristan can take it. Give me a couple of

minutes." Froggy hustled away, yelling at a girl climbing on the pool table.

"Hey, I said I wanted a beer. You could have at least ordered me one." Maddox sighed.

"You could have piped in and ordered one, but you were zoned out and didn't think of it. So you get what I say you can have."

"Wow. Your boyfriend is suffering, and instead of being sympathetic and taking care of me, you shove fruity drinks at me."

Tristan shrugged. "Figured it'll help you loosen up and relax a bit. You're scowling and it's scaring the other customers."

Jaylen laughed as he glanced around the busy bar. "I know you guys have said it before, but are you sure it's okay for me to be here? Some of these people are giving me odd looks. If I have to pee, is it safe to go alone, or should one of you hold my hand?"

"Phew, I thought you were going to ask us to hold something else." Maddox winked. "You are with us so no one will mess with you and everyone saw Froggy being friendly with you and he is King here. No one will cross him and risk getting banned."

Jaylen blew out a breath and nodded. "Good to

know." He looked at the bar and studied Froggy. "He doesn't seem like he could hold his own against some of the patrons in here. What is he anyway?"

"It has nothing to do with physical strength. They aren't going to risk him cutting them off. He makes the cheapest, best drinks in the area. No one wants to get kicked out by him."

Tristan cocked his head. "You know I don't know what he is either. I'm still learning the rules, but is it bad etiquette to ask?" He laughed, "Have a drink Jaylen and then you can ask because he won't kill you for being drunk."

Maddox shook his head. "Look at the agent and cop, scared of a little bartender." He nodded at Froggy as he set the drinks down on the table. "These gentlemen here are afraid to ask what kind of supe you are."

Froggy shot his tongue out real fast. "Isn't it obvious by my name?"

Jaylen's jaw dropped. "All of you fits into a tiny little frog or are you like a giant frog the size of a recliner?"

All three paranormals cocked their heads and gave him odd looks.

Froggy shook his head. "I'm just kidding man, I'm a Titan."

Jaylen picked up his glass and took a sip and promptly began choking. "Holy hell. This is good, but strong. Did I get the right glass? This is the one made for the mere human, right?"

Tristan laughed and raised his glass to Froggy. "A Titan, that's pretty awesome. I don't know much about your kind other than what I know from Disney's Hercules."

Froggy grabbed the drink from Tristan's hand. "Just for that, no drink for you. That movie made us look like assholes." He turned and took three steps before coming back. "Just kidding. Here's your drink. I love that movie. Those singing muses are great."

Jaylen giggled as he took a big sip of his drink and started dancing in his seat. "I love this song."

Tristan eyed the nearly empty glass, "Uh, I don't think you're supposed to drink it that fast man."

"Shut it. That shit is awesome. Come dance with me, if your man doesn't mind, of course." Jaylen turned his pleading eyes to Maddox. "Can I dance with him? I promise it's innocent."

Maddox made a face as he choked down the sweet mixture. "Have at him. I need you to burn some of his energy so I can get some sleep when we get home. Boy can't keep his hands to himself when we're alone."

"You're sleeping alone tonight," Tristan grumbled as he allowed Jaylen to pull him up from the seat. "And order me another drink. I'm going to need it."

Four songs later, Tristan and Jaylen threw themselves back into the booth. "Oh my god, that felt good. I can't remember the last time I danced that much." Jaylen sucked from the straw of his empty cup.

Maddox slid a drink over to Tristan. "Here you go, sloppy seconds."

Tristan laughed, "Um, is that the name of the drink or because you don't want it?"

"Technically, you are Jaylen's sloppy seconds because you were here with me first. But to answer your question, it's the name of the drink. I don't ask Froggy why he names them the way he does. I'm not sure I want to know."

"And here's a baby sloppy second for you." He pushed a smaller glass over to Jaylen.

"Oh, that's good." Tristan said as he took a big gulp. "I don't care what it's called, I want another." He stood and waved to Froggy and pointed to his rapidly emptying glass.

Maddox sighed. "I'm going to end up carrying both of you out of here, aren't I?"

Jaylen shrugged as he studied the room. "I bet I could find someone to carry me so you can focus on your man."

Froggy came over with four glasses. "I brought two each for you guys, so I don't have to come over here as much."

"Really?" Maddox yelled at his retreating back. "I just want a beer. I think he's holding out on purpose. But he doesn't mind pumping you guys with this crap." He grabbed a slice of pineapple from his cup and popped it in his mouth.

"Let's leave grumpy pants to stew and go dance some more." Jaylen called as he jumped to his feet and swayed a bit. "I'm having so much fun."

An hour later, Maddox was taking slow, heavy steps across the parking lot. "You guys aren't exactly light, you know." A very drunk Tristan and Jaylen were each slung over one of his shoulders, singing at the top of their lungs. "Froggy did offer to help with you, Jaylen."

"No! It's not fair. If you were going to carry Tristan, I wanted to be carried too. I've never been held by an ogre before." He hiccupped.

Tristan giggled, "But Froggy's a Titan. He's strong too."

"But I don't know him." Jaylen whispered loudly. "And Maddox smells good."

Tristan nodded as he slapped Maddox's ass that was in his face. "But he's mine, so don't get ideas."

"Now who's the party pooper?" Jaylen stuck his tongue out at him.

"If you two are done, get in the back of Jaylen's car. I'm not putting either of you in Scarlet." He groaned as he bent down and lifted them off his shoulders.

Tristan rolled his eyes. "See, he loves Scarlet more than me. He's always putting her first."

"I've never been secretive about that." Maddox said matter-of-factly as he opened the back door and shoved Tristan inside. "Why did I do this to myself? I could have just had a cold beer at home in the silence. Instead, I'm here with the peanut gallery." He muttered as he walked Jaylen around the car and put him in the other side.

"You can sleep in my room with me, Jaylen. The jackass up there can sleep alone."

Maddox climbed behind the wheel. "Ha. We both know how you get when you're drunk. You can't keep it in your pants. Even if I locked my bedroom door, you'd find a way to get inside."

Tristan frowned as he turned to stare out the window. "Not tonight. I'm mad at you."

"Why is the car spinning?" Jaylen asked with his head back, staring at the roof of the car. "Tristan, Tristan, look, we're spinning."

"Oh god, no." Tristan exclaimed. "Are you trying to make me throw up in your car?"

"I draw the line at cleaning up vomit, so think twice about doing that." Maddox shouted over his shoulder.

Jaylen shrugged. "I'll sell it as is."

"There are probably a few paranormals that might enjoy that." Maddox glanced at them in the mirror. When they both gagged, he threw his head back and laughed.

He pulled into their assigned parking spot. "Okay guys, you made it home."

Jaylen's head flopped to the side. "Why am I here again?"

Maddox sighed as he opened the door and pulled the tiny human out. "You drank a lot of alcohol and you live alone. I don't want to be responsible for you choking on your own vomit. That's all we need, a human dying from drinking in a supe bar."

He leaned Jayden on the car and used his leg to

hold him up while he opened the door. He helped Tristan up, who then threw his arms around his neck and kissed his cheek. "You are so smart." He flopped against the car and leaned toward Jaylen. "He's smart, don't you think? And gorgeous."

Maddox blew out a breath. This was not how he thought the night would go. He bent down and threw each one over a shoulder and headed inside as they continued bantering about all his amazing qualities.

He pushed Tristan's ass against the wall to help balance him while he unlocked the door. God, what he would give for a doorbell camera at this moment.

It was slow going, but he got to Tristan's room. "Does anyone need to use the bathroom before you go to bed?"

"We don't all have to go together, do we?" Jaylen asked.

"Are you asking us to hold something again?" Tristan asked.

Maddox sat them down on the bed. "I'm going to get you guy's water. Bathroom is there, and the bed is underneath you."

He left them singing again. Lord, they had more energy than he'd ever had in his life.

When he came back with the two glasses, both

men were curled up sleeping. He set the cups on the side table and bent over to pick up Tristan. Tristan's eyes opened a bit. "What's going on?"

"You're mine. You sleep with me."

Tristan nodded, "Okay. Love you."

Maddox smiled as Tristan fell back to sleep. He loved his phoenix too.

CHAPTER
Twenty-Three

TRISTAN ROLLED OVER AND GROANED, "Fuck, my head hurts. Why did we drink so much?"

Jaylen grunted as he passed by in the hallway. "I need someone to kill me, please."

Maddox leaned against the counter, sipping his coffee. He smiled at them over his mug. "I don't know what you guys are talking about. I feel great."

"Fuck off." Tristan grumbled as he tried to climb out of bed. "I think I'm going to throw up. Remind me to never drink again."

"Froggy will be very disappointed to hear that. I'm not sure you want to upset him." Maddox innocently shrugged.

"I'll be okay if I don't see him any time soon."

Jaylen called out right before he shut the guest bathroom door.

Tristan wanted to laugh, but he knew better. He could only imagine how bad Jaylen must be if he felt like death and he was kind of used to the shifter drinks. For a human to match him glass for glass was damn impressive.

"If you princesses could hurry up, we need to get to the office. I'll just be in here making eggs, and maybe some greasy bacon. Do you guys want some?" Maddox chuckled quietly, waiting for their responses.

"Bastard." Tristan yelled out as he slammed the door closed and then winced as his head pounded even more. He quickly stripped out of the clothes he'd slept in and jumped in the shower, not caring if it was completely warmed up yet.

As he let the water beat down on his head, he tried to recall everything that had happened the night before. Too much of it was a blur. He remembered dancing and lots of drinking, but why did he feel like something big had happened? He frowned as the memory slipped through his fingers.

He tried to piece things together as he finished and got dressed. He blew out a breath of frustration as he made his way to the coffeepot and the biggest cup he could find.

"Morning." Jaylen greeted softly from his place at the table.

Tristan turned and smiled at the sight of their friend with his head laying on the tabletop. "Guess I should count my blessings. I'm not quite as bad off as you are."

Maddox patted Tristan's shoulder. "Give it another hour and you'll be feeling much better. Shifters don't have hangovers for long."

Jaylen scowled at them. "Somehow, that isn't fair. I shouldn't have drank so much. How am I going to fake my way through the day?"

"It's just manning the tip line. That should make you feel better. You love talking to the people."

Jaylen groaned. "Maybe I'll just call out sick. I'll say I have a stomach bug."

Tristan snickered, "Want me to call in for you and tell them you're stuck in the bathroom and can't make the call?"

"I love you guys, but I'm not ready for everyone to know I slept over here. I'm already a bit of a pariah. I'd like to keep some semblance of the status quo."

Maddox snapped his fingers. "Damn, and here I

wanted to say you were in bed with us when you felt sick and had to run to the bathroom and haven't been able to come out."

Jaylen cocked an eyebrow. "If you were human, who says they'd have batted an eye at that? Maybe it's a common occurrence for me to be in men's beds..." He laughed as they shared a look before studying him.

"You're really not going to tell us your sexuality because dude, I've been trying to figure it out since I met you." Tristan nodded in agreement with Maddox.

Jaylen shrugged. "Nah. I like to keep people guessing. It adds to the mystery."

"Fine, keep your secrets." Tristan grinned. "But I'm going to be watching you and see who you react to. You know this is a safe place, right? We won't judge you... much."

"Sure." Jaylen laughed good-naturedly as he moved to refill his coffee. "It's my car, so I say we can have food and drinks in it."

"I'm not sure I'm up to food just yet." Tristan winced as he rubbed his stomach. "Are you seriously hungry?"

Maddox chuckled as he popped a bunch of slices of bread into the four slot toaster. "I'll make you some toast, whiny baby. That should help some."

Tristan pouted at his boyfriend. "Why are you being so mean to me?"

Jaylen grinned as he looked between the two of them. "Not to interrupt, but I have a question I'm dying to know the answer to."

"Should we be worried?" Tristan asked as he brought his mug over for a refill. "I love you man, but some things are meant to be private."

"Apparently, I was in your bed last night." Jaylen smirked. "Doesn't get much more private than that. But that actually is what I wanted to ask. Why in the hell do you guys have separate bedrooms?"

Maddox rolled his eyes. "What is it with you people? We've known each other for like two months. It makes sense we'd have our own private spaces for when we need them. Just because we're gay doesn't mean we get married immediately after meeting."

"Who said anything about marriage? You live together, so it's a logical question." Jaylen defended. "I'm sorry it's such a touchy subject."

"Tallie has been on us constantly about it, too. She has a one track mind."

Tristan grinned at Maddox as he replied to

Jaylen, "Doesn't help that he had a bit of a commitment phobia. He's making progress. Give him a break."

Maddox dumped the last sip of coffee down the drain and rinsed his mug. "If you two are done, we need to go. Jaylen needs to get on those phone lines."

"Ugh. Fine. I can do this." Jaylen blew out a breath and turned his head from side to side, cracking his neck.

"Are you going to work out?" Maddox asked.

"No. I'm pumping myself up. You guys don't do that?"

Tristan snickered. "I pump something up."

Jaylen groaned, "Are you sure you matured past middle school?"

Tristan laughed as he grabbed his wallet and keys from the counter and headed to the front door. "We can take my truck and get Scarlet after work, unless you want to go now?"

"Froggy won't let anything happen to my car. She'll be safe there for the day." Maddox mumbled with a full mouth of dry toast.

Tristan nodded as he pushed the button for the elevator. Suddenly, he stiffened as a flashback from the night before came to him. He'd said he loved Maddox. Had that been a dream, or had it really happened? Wouldn't Maddox have said something or maybe freaked out if it'd been real? He peaked at Maddox and bit his lip. How could he figure it out without admitting anything? He did love him, but he wasn't sure Maddox was ready to hear that. Hell, he wasn't sure if Maddox felt the same way or not, and it wasn't like he was brave enough to ask him outright. He was hung over, not stupid.

Tristan's phone vibrated in the cup holder.

Maddox grabbed his at the same time. "Vic says to head to the TPD 22nd Street office. We're going to have a joint meeting to go over tips."

Tristan frowned. "Why there and not back at One Police Plaza like yesterday?"

They pulled in next to Jaylen.

"Long time no see. Guess you guys got the message, too."

"It's probably Detective Dickhead flexing by making us come to him." Maddox sneered as he followed Jayden in the building.

Tristan snickered as he trailed after them, memories of his years in the building flashing in his mind. He'd thought he'd retire from this building, and instead, a few short years later, he'd been kicked to the curb and left to rot.

He kept his head up as he walked the halls, but was careful to avoid meeting any of the detective's eyes. He wasn't in the mood to put up with any of their shit today.

Maddox leaned close to Jaylen. "If you see Tristan's old partner, point him out to me. I want to see what the douche bag looks like."

Jaylen snorted as he shook his head. "Are you going to have a pissing contest with another TPD detective?"

"Ha," Maddox shot back arrogantly, "There is no contest. Their puny dicks are no match for mine."

"Thankfully, I've never seen his to comment, but from his long line of girlfriends, and the rumors floating around the precinct.... You'd win, no contest." Tristan wiggled his pinky finger.

They made their way to the conference room, where Vic was waiting with his arms crossed over his massive chest and a scowl on his face. "Why do you two look like shit? What kind of impression does that make on these idiots?"

Jaylen frowned. "Hey, I work with them and don't give a shit. But yeah Tristan, what's your deal?"

Tristan flipped him off. "You shouldn't have kept me up all last night then."

Vic glanced between them. "You're a throuple now?"

Jaylen groaned as he rolled his eyes. "No, he only wishes he could get in my pants. I slept alone for the record."

Detective Dickhead walked in and went to the end of the long conference table. "Morning everyone. Let's get started." He waited for everyone to get seated. Some of the detectives eyed them wearily, trying to figure out where to sit so they weren't too close to them.

"I think I might lick all the door handles before we leave." Maddox whispered.

"Don't even fucking think about it." Vic growled back.

Tristan leaned forward to whisper in Maddox's ear. "I'll distract him while you go lick."

Before Vic could snap at them again, the meeting started. "We received over fourteen hundred tips since the press conference. Ninety percent were just batshit crazies. We've had twenty tips that were credible enough that we started running them down immediately. At seven this morning, a guy came in and gave us video footage from the GoPro he wears on his helmet when he's riding his motorcycle. Based on the story and location, my guess is he was street racing, so he refused to give his personal information."

Detective Dickhead grabbed a remote and pointed it at a screen. The video started with the person wearing the camera talking to another guy sitting on his motorcycle. After a few seconds, the guy and the camera both turn and look off to the right. An ambulance pulled in, then several seconds later, another car pulled up. A man got out of the ambulance while a second man got out of the car. They got in each other's faces, arms flailing back and forth, appearing to be arguing. After another minute, the men grabbed gas cans out of the trunk of the car, doused the ambulance inside and out, and then set it on fire.

"Holy shit." Tristan whispered as he leaned forward. "Is there any chance we can zoom in on their faces? Because if I'm not mistaken, the man in the car is our missing Dr. Rogers."

"We're already working on that and should have the information shortly." Detective Dickhead replied, before turning his back on Tristan. "There is no clear picture of the license plate on the car, unfortunately."

The door of the conference room swung open. A cop in uniform handed a piece of paper to the detective and walked out.

He read the note. "Interesting. A Dr. Fred Hamlin called in to say he's been out of the country. He received a call from his home alarm company. It turned out his friend Dr. Brian Rogers has been staying at his house and accidentally set the alarm off. Dr. Hamlin didn't know anything about the disappearance until a friend sent him a link to watch the press conference."

Vic smiled as he pulled out his phone and typed a message, "I'll have Cole pull some surveillance and see if he can get proof that our missing Doctor really is there."

Chief Barlowe cleared his throat to get everyone's attention. "Vic, you guys have better equipment than we have access to and less red tape. If we get you a copy of the GoPro tape, can you guys look into getting IDs on our two men?"

Vic nodded. "Absolutely, if you can have it sent to this email." He jotted Cole's address on a piece of paper and slid it across the table. "Cole can do it and probably have an answer by the time this meeting closes."

Detective Dickhead pushed another button, and

a list came up. "While we're waiting for results, let's go over the other nineteen credible tips."

Tristan yawned as he stood in front of the coffeepot in the TPD detective's lounge as he waited for it to finish brewing. "This is the meeting that won't end." He grumbled.

Jaylen nodded. "Dude, my ears are bleeding, I think. Why do we have to debate every freaking tip to death? Less talking, more action."

"I bet that's what all your dates tell you too." Tristan jumped out of the way as Jaylen laughed and swatted at him playfully.

"If you kids are done goofing off, Cole just called in with some information." Vic announced from the doorway with a shake of his head. "I swear it's like herding toddlers."

Tristan repeated his words in a mocking tone as he quickly poured his coffee. "And he only ever says that when Maddox isn't around. But we all know he's the biggest instigator, too."

Jaylen laughed as he nudged him out of the way so he could get a cup. "Come on, let's see what's happening. Maybe we'll get lucky and it'll be enough to end the hours of torture."

"You know this should be against the Geneva convention or something." Tristan grumbled as he made his way back down the hallway.

Maddox stood along the windows, looking out over the city. Several feet away, a group was standing together, staring at him and whispering. The leader of the pack was none other than Tristan's ex-partner.

Tristan paused in the doorway and took in the scene before moving up next to Maddox and bumping his shoulder against his. "Hey gorgeous, fancy meeting you here." He said loud enough for the group of detectives to hear him. "I was thinking that maybe tomorrow we could practice flying some, but you'll have to do your thing to make my wings pop, big guy."

Maddox turned and lifted an eyebrow. "I thought we were past that. I've seen your wings pop in and out easily." Then he noticed the group watching them. He stepped closer to Tristan. "But I'm happy to smack your ass whenever you want." He caressed Tristan's cheek, then walked past him to go back to the conference room.

Tristan shuddered at the sensation and then had to

hide his laugh as he heard the whispering get louder at their display. Assholes never had an issue with him being gay, but now that he wasn't human, they had an issue with everything he did. Good thing he didn't care what they thought. He turned and smiled at them as he followed his partner back into the meeting.

Vic was standing in the front of the room with the Chief beside him. "I've gotten word back from our computer expert." He gestured to the screen. "This is the blown up picture of our two suspects. He's been able to successfully ID Dr. Rogers as the man from the car. He's still working on the second man, though."

"This is enough for us to get a warrant for his arrest," Chief Barlowe added.

"Without going into any details," Vic glanced at the humans then back at Maddox and Tristan, "we've also been able to see Dr. Hamlin's camera feed and Cole confirmed Dr. Rogers is there with the man from the other video and a woman who was likely the one pretending to be the paramedic when they picked up Quinn Rogers. While we wait for the warrant to come in, I'll call the rest of my team and have them meet us here." He pulled a map up on the screen and pointed at a parking lot a block away from the neighborhood. "Let's gear up."

An hour later, they were in their assigned teams and driving to their designated parking areas. Maddox, Tristan, Detective Dickhead, and his partner were the team going in the front door.

"I still don't understand why we didn't bring swat in to breach the door." The young detective whispered.

Maddox and Tristan looked at each other and smiled as they both lifted one leg and kicked the door in. Shards of wood flew as the door was splintered.

At the same time Maddox called out P.I.S. there was a crash in the back of the house as someone yelled Police.

Detective Dickhead groaned as he followed them in the door, "Don't tell anyone I breached with P.I.S.."

PART
Two

CHAPTER
Twenty~Four

THREE WEEKS earlier

Dr. Brian Rogers wanted to throw up. The police that came to the lab and picked him up only said his daughter was in an accident. He didn't know the extent, he just knew he couldn't lose her. It'd only been a few years since he'd lost his wife. Quinn was smiling again, and they were talking about taking a vacation. Life was finally getting back to normal.

The officers led him through the emergency room where a doctor was waiting for them. Brian's hand shook as he reached out to shake the doctors.

"Dr. Rogers, I'm Dr. Fellows. Before we go inside, I need you to prepare yourself. There was an incident downtown and your daughter's car was crushed, pinning her inside. She has extensive crush injuries, blood loss, and burns over thirty percent of her body. She's in an extremely critical condition and her chances of survival aren't great. We have her stabilized enough now to move her up to the burn unit."

Brian felt his knees shake as he began to collapse. The officer caught him and held him up as he felt his heart shatter at the news.

"We have her under IV sedation, so remember she won't be able to see you or talk to you, but she can hear and feel you."

Brian nodded and then steadied himself as he followed the doctor into the room. The sound of the ventilator reached his ears before he saw her. The overpowering smell of antiseptic, a sour liquor mixed with soap combination, that after all his years in the hospital you'd think he'd be used to, assaulted his nose.

She looked tiny in the middle of the bed, surrounded by machines and bandages covering large portions of her body.

"My god, my baby girl." He sobbed as he shuffled closer to the bed. He wanted to hold her, to know she was okay, but he knew even the smallest touch would cause her excruciating pain.

All his years of medical practice still didn't prepare him to see her like this. He knew what every machine was for, everything they were going to have to do, but none of it brought him comfort. He also knew what pain was coming her way, and he'd give anything to protect her from that.

"How did this happen?" He demanded as he hovered over his little girl. "Why her?" He whimpered as he dropped into the chair by the bed.

The police officer who had held him up pulled out a notebook. "There was a fight between two paranormals. Your daughter was driving down the road and got caught in the middle. The creatures landed on her car, crushing her inside."

"Are they here? Are they as hurt as she is?" Was it petty to hope they were suffering as bad as she was? When your child was the one injured, petty was the least of your concerns.

The police officer shook his head. "They flew away. Both Tampa PD and the Paranormal Investigative Services are searching for them. There were numerous casualties. The victims were sent to a few different hospitals."

Dr. Fellows walked up next to the bed. "We're

ready to move her upstairs. She'll be on the sixth floor of the West Pavilion in room C622 in the burn unit. Why don't you go ahead and wait up there while we get her situated?"

A nurse walked up and handed him a plastic white bag. "Here are your daughters' personal items."

He nodded as he made his way out of the room. The police officer followed him to the elevators. "I'm very sorry you're going through this. Is there anyone we can call for you?"

Brian shook his head. "She's all I've got."

He stood there, hugging the bag to his chest.

The officer pushed the button for the elevator for him. "A detective will be in touch with you to keep you up to date on the case."

Brian nodded numbly and shuffled into the elevator. The overwhelming heaviness in his body made him break out in a cold sweat, with tingling running through his veins. The ride up six floors was over too soon. He followed the signs to the room number he was given.

A young woman in scrubs walked up and smiled at him. "Are you the family of Quinn Rogers?"

He nodded.

"The team is bringing her up now. If you can stay

out here while we get her settled, that will help."

She pointed to a single chair a few feet away. "You can wait over there."

She walked back to the nurse's station. He'd never felt so alone in his life. He sat in the chair, his leg bouncing nervously. Every time he heard the elevator ding he would jump up, then deflate when it wasn't her.

What felt like an eternity later, six people stepped off the elevator, escorting Quinn and all her machines down the hall. Even with his medical knowledge, he was still shocked to see how much was required to keep her alive. Between the ventilator and multiple infusion pumps, there were more wires and tubes than people treating her.

The doctor from downstairs nodded at him as they passed. "We'll let you in as soon as she's settled in."

The nurse who greeted him followed them in. He didn't realize he was holding his breath until he heard the compression of the ventilator breathe for her. Subconsciously, he matched rhythm with it.

One by one, the transport team left. The young nurse stepped out of the door and waved for him to come in.

He took a deep breath. The bag of her personal

items still pressed against his chest.

"Take your time." She stepped back and let him through the door.

He took his time taking in his surroundings. The doctor side of him took over as he evaluated her condition. He noted the ventilator settings and winced at the amount of support she needed. Logically, he knew she needed a lot of pressure support because of her crush injuries and because of her collapsed lungs that they'd had to re-inflate with chest tubes. He was well aware of the effect this kind of trauma could have on her liver. It would be a fight to keep it from becoming congested and falter, if not fail. Her small body would struggle to handle the extreme amount of fluid and blood needed due to the burns. His eyes filled with large pools of tears just thinking of the pain she would endure to treat the burns. He checked the monitors to see how her vital signs were with the move upstairs. Her heart rhythm was rapid, but mostly normal. The blood pressure was low, but the medication was keeping her mean pressure above sixty, protecting her kidney's for now. Nausea overwhelmed him, knowing this was going to be the fight of a lifetime. The odds of total organ failure were weighing on his mind, and dread consumed him.

The nurse came back in and checked each monitor, writing down the levels. "Is there anything I can get you? Would you like the chaplain to come in?"

He glanced up at her. "I apologize. I didn't get your name?"

She looked up from her paper and smiled at him. "I'm Gina and I'll be with you for the next ten hours."

He nodded. "Thank you, Gina. I don't need anything right now. The chaplain won't be necessary." He cleared his throat. "I'm sure you can't answer this, but what are the odds she beats this?"

She put her pen down and faced him. "I heard you're in the medical field?"

"Yes. I was a medical examiner, then moved to pathology at St. Bernadette's."

She nodded. "Okay. So, you know this will be a long battle with many issues to overcome. There's a strong likelihood of infection, blood clots, and RSV from long-term ventilator use. Everything will be complicated by her organs trying to recover on top of the muscle and tissue loss. We're going to do everything we can to make this as easy a process as possible."

Gina walked around the bed and pulled aside the blanket. She gently pulled Quinn's arm out and tucked the blanket back. "As long as you don't move her too much, you can hold her hand."

Tears welled in his eyes at seeing her limp hand. He shook as he reached up and gently grasped her fingers with his. At the angle he was sitting at, it was all he could do without hurting her. He laid his forehead against their clasped hands and let the tears fall. How did he let this happen to his baby girl?

Brian was gently shaken awake. A new nurse was standing over him. "Morning. I'm Clara. I'll be Quinn's nurse today. The overnight nurse walked me through everything. We're going to be changing her bandages, so if you want to go down to the cafeteria or run home and get clothes, we'll be busy with her for about an hour."

"Okay. Maybe I'll run home and grab some of her things to have in here for when she wakes up." For his mental health, he had to believe that was going to be any minute.

While he drove home, his mind raced with all the medical care she was going to need over the next few months. It was ironic that he hadn't gotten rid of any of the medical supplies from when they took care of his wife, and now he'd need them for their daughter.

He raced through the house, packing a duffel bag as fast as possible. Even with rushing, it still took an hour and a half to get to the house and back. Damn Tampa traffic.

Clara stepped out of the room as he walked off the elevator. "Good timing. Dr. Brumfield is in there if you want to get an update."

He thanked her and walked quickly into the room. "Morning Dr. Brumfield. Sorry I missed you last night. When we spoke last, you said there were no changes. Do you have good news today?"

"We attempted to bring her up from the deep sedation to assess her neurological function, but not so much to cause her pain level to get too high. We were able to decrease the sedation quite a bit. We're a little concerned as she has shown little reaction to the pain. She is requiring more pressure support and her blood pressure has been fluctuating. But overall, she is stable."

"Are you thinking organ failure, or is this just her body's response to the trauma?" Brian asked as his mind went into doctor mode. He had to compartmentalize, or he'd never get through this without breaking down and they wouldn't speak as freely to him.

"She's critical but stable. We need to be cautious about how much her body has been through and whether she's going to be able to overcome everything."

Brian knew what Dr. Brumfield wasn't saying. Her recovery was almost insurmountable. He waited until the other man had left before sinking into the chair and letting the tears fall. Without saying it outright, they were warning him she wasn't likely to make it through. He was going to lose his baby girl just like he'd lost his wife. He'd failed them both.

Gina walked in with a muffin. "Morning Dr. Rogers. One of the doctors had a bunch of pastries delivered, so I grabbed this for you."

He took the blueberry muffin with a smile. "Thank you, I appreciate it."

"Dr. Brumfield is right behind me. We can go over the latest labs."

A few seconds later, the smiling doctor walked in. "Morning." Brian sat quietly while Dr. Brumfield reviewed the chart, monitors, and vent settings.

After a few minutes, he grabbed the rolling stool and sat across from Brian. "I'm concerned her condition is not improving. Her labs show multi-organ deterioration. Her liver function shows it's failing, the kidneys are not putting out urine and her respiratory status has also declined. She has developed a fever which, while expected, is quite alarming because her white blood cell count is extremely elevated."

"Okay. That's not great, but we can get past this. She's young and strong. What's the plan from here? What about dialysis? If we improve her kidney function, that should improve everything else, right?" He tried to keep his voice calm while inside, the panic was threatening to suffocate him. He couldn't let them give up on her.

Dr. Brumfield sighed, "Dialysis is indicated but there will be major risks because her blood pressure is so low and there's a concern that she will have a heart attack with her anemia."

Brian nodded eagerly. "She's going to die without it, right? So let's try it."

Dr. Brumfield gave Gina a look, then turned back to Brian. "Okay. It'll take some time to get everything set up and get the machine up here."

Brian reached out his hand to shake the doctors.

"Thank you. I know how frustrating medical people can be as family members. I appreciate your candor and willingness to listen to me."

"We all want what's best for your daughter." He nodded at him and left the room.

Sitting alone with Quinn, listening to the ventilator, he knew he needed to come up with a plan B in case they asked him about palliative care. No way was he doing that. His girl was strong. She would fight this. He wouldn't, couldn't give up on her. He may have had a moment of weakness the day before, but he was back today and he wasn't going to let her slip away. He'd fight for her until she was ready to do it on her own.

He grabbed his phone to research options. It was a race against the clock now.

The salamander is unique in that it's capable of regenerating lost limbs as well as other damaged parts of their bodies. Researchers hope to reverse engineer the regenerative processes for potential human medical applications such as brain and spinal cord injury treatment or preventing harmful scarring during heart surgery recovery.

Dr. Brumfield knocked on the door frame of the room. Brian muted the t.v. ."Morning, come on in."

Dr. Brumfield smiled sadly and moved to sit across from him. "Our critical care team has met and evaluated your daughter's case. She has continued to deteriorate despite treatment and the dialysis only slightly improved her kidney function. We feel she is at a point where palliative care needs to be considered. She has shown no signs of waking up or improvement in her organ failure. We all agree she has no chance of recovery. We want you to consider making her a DNR."

Brian shook his head. "Absolutely not. I knew this was coming. I've talked with an acute long-term facility. They can have a spot open for her in two days. I just need you to take care of her until their ambulance comes to transfer her."

Dr. Brumfield shook his head sadly. "You have to understand she will not get better. I want to caution you that the move alone may be too much for her frail body."

Brian nodded his understanding. "I'm willing to take that risk. I appreciate everything you have done for her. Your whole team has been fantastic." He looked down at Quinn. "While you're changing the bandages, I'm going to run by the facility and make sure everything is in order."

Brumfield sighed. "Okay. I'll let the nurses know you'll be out for a while."

Once he was alone, he leaned close to Quinn and whispered in her ear. "Don't worry, baby girl. Daddy's gonna save you."

He grabbed his phone and texted a number, then grabbed his keys and left. They may have given up on Quinn, but he never would.

Twenty minutes later, he sat at a picnic bench watching ducks swim in a pond. He waved at the man walking toward him. "Greg. Good to see you." He shook hands with the tall, thin man. "It's been a long time." He had worked with him years ago, but the anesthesiologist was caught using drugs and fired. He never kicked the habit and rumor was he was now an underground doc, fixing up people who couldn't or wouldn't go to a real hospital. And Brian chose the facility because Greg's girlfriend worked there and also had a drug problem. They should be easy enough to convince to help him for the right price.

"I admit I was surprised to get your call." He sat down across from Brian.

Brian pulled an envelope out of a bag. "This is

ten thousand dollars. I need you to work with me for a couple of weeks and when it's over, I'll give you another fifteen thousand."

Greg opened the envelope and flipped through the stack of hundreds and twenties. "It must be bad if you need to offer me this much."

"We're going to need Christina too."

Greg nodded. "If we agree to the job, it'll cost another five thousand to include her."

Brian scowled at the other man. "Fine. But I'm still only giving ten until the job is done." He slid a piece of paper over. "Tampa Medical Center called Christina's facility and set up a transport. I need Christina to go in and change the pickup time from eight a.m. to ten a.m. Before the transfer, I need you to steal an ambulance from this company. Their trucks are equipped for our needs. You'll need to be dressed as paramedics and go to the hospital to pick my daughter up and say you are transporting her back to Christina's facility. I want your girl-friend to drive so you can be in the back. Quinn is on a ventilator. She's on hypotensive agents and sedated. She has extensive crush and burn injuries, so you'll have to drive carefully. I need you to make sure she stays alive while you drive her to this address."

Greg's eyes were wide. "Jesus man. That is horrible. How old is she?"

"She turned eighteen two months ago. She was going to be leaving for USF in the fall." He blinked away the tears.

He shook off the emotion and continued with the plan. "Use this code to open the garage door. Inside will be a transport van. You'll need to move Quinn from the ambulance to the van and empty all the equipment and supplies you can from the ambulance. Then you'll drive to this address and park inside the garage to avoid as many people seeing you as possible. This is the key to the house and the code for the alarm. I'm going to have to put on a scene about her disappearing and deal with the cops, but I'll get to the house as soon as I can. Good so far?"

Greg stared at him for a few seconds. "This is a lot of felonies for thirty thousand. I'm weighing the pros and cons."

Brian slammed his hand on the picnic table. "You will be helping to save a young girl's life and you're getting thirty thousand in cash that you can do whatever you want with."

"Fine. What else do I need to know?"

Brian blew out a relieved breath. "Once we're in the house, the three of us will be on round-the-clock care taking care of her until she is stable enough that I can take care of her on my own. I am going to need some supplies to keep her comfortable and to treat her."

Greg folded his arms across his chest. "And what happens to us if she dies?"

Brian glared and shook his head vehemently, "Nothing, because she isn't going to die."

Greg snorted but hadn't taken his eyes off the stack of money. "Okay. We'll do it. If it goes more than a month, we want more money."

Brian nodded his agreement. He didn't know where he'd come up with thousands more, but he'd do anything for her. "I need to run another errand before I go back to the hospital. Do you want to text me your list?"

"No. I have a lot of supplies and Christina steals from the facility when I get low on something."

"Perfect, she'll need pain meds, so I was thinking it'll be easy if we make a Brompton Solution. Can you get cocaine and morphine? I'll take care of the rest."

"Is that still used? I thought it went out back in the 70's."

"It did, but it works well and I think she's going

to need something really strong to help get through this."

Greg nodded, "Consider it done, also I have someone I trust that can steal the ambulance and won't say a word. And I have a contact for blood, too."

Brian sagged in relief. "That is excellent to hear. It was one of the few items on my list I was struggling to find a way to get."

"Vampires are great resources for blood, so it's easy to get."

"Vampires?" Brian blanched. "Is that safe?"

Greg nodded, "I've used him for a while. It's safe and he's never let me down. If you want me to go someplace else, it's going to take time."

Brian frowned. "No, time isn't on our side. It'll have to be him."

Both men stood and shook hands. "Good luck tomorrow. I'm trusting you with my daughter's life."

Greg used the envelope of money to salute him, then turned and left.

He walked back to his car, feeling lighter. If this hadn't worked out, he didn't have another plan and this one was crazy enough. There was no turning back now. But no matter what, she was worth this and so much more.

CHAPTER
Twenty-Five

BRIAN PULLED into the parking lot of the police station. He took a deep breath and steeled himself for the performance of his lifetime. With the detective's card in hand, he waited his turn to check in.

"Morning, can I help you?" The patrolman barely glanced up from his computer.

He slid the card across the desk. "This detective is investigating my daughter's case. I wanted to talk with him and get an update."

The cop glanced at the table, then picked up his phone. "Let me see if he's available. You can have a seat over there."

Brian took the card back and sat next to a woman with black eyes and a bandaged arm.

About the time Brian was losing his nerve and going to leave, a man came out and called his name. "Dr. Rogers?"

He held his hand up and walked over to him.

"Morning. I'm Detective Franklin. Why don't we go into a conference room and we can talk?"

Brian followed him through the hallways. Sweat ran down his back. There was no way any of them knew what was happening over at the hospital this very moment, but he still felt like there was a big neon sign above him blinking *kidnapper*.

Detective Franklin opened a door and pointed inside. "Do you want a coffee or water?"

"No, thank you. I had breakfast at the hospital before I left."

The older man sat across from him and opened a file. "We don't have much for you right now. We've been able to identify the two men, but both are on the run. The Paranormal Agency is involved and leading the manhunt. We have some leads we're following, so we're hopeful we'll have them in hand soon."

Brian nodded solemnly. "One of the nurses mentioned bystanders were waiting with Quinn while they waited for the first responders. Do you have their names? I'd like to thank them."

The detective flipped through a couple of papers. "I have a husband and wife listed as the ones who stayed with her until the firemen arrived. I can give them your contact information and they can reach out if they want to."

Brian took a pen and pad of paper from the detective. "This is my cell number and my email. Let them know I'm grateful for what they did and want to thank them."

"Absolutely. How's your daughter doing?"

Brian's throat constricted. He had to be careful to keep his story straight. "Actually, we're having her transferred today. The hospital feels there is no hope for recovery, so I'm having her moved to a private facility where I can make her more comfortable and let her friends visit while we wait for her to heal."

The detective shook his head. "That is terrible. So many families have been devastated by these animals who had no business on our side of town."

Brian took the anger inside himself and locked it away. There would be time later to be angry at the ones responsible. Right now, he needed to focus on Quinn. "I appreciate you taking the time to talk with me. I look forward to good news soon on the manhunt."

After he was safely back in the car, he checked

his cell phone. An unknown number texted that the package was in hand. He laid his forehead on the steering wheel and let the tears fall. So far, so good.

Brian stood at the receptionist's desk, waiting for the woman to get off the phone. His hands were in his pockets to hide how much he was shaking.

She hung up and smiled up at him. "Sorry to keep you waiting. Can I help you?"

"I'm Dr. Brian Rogers. My daughter was picked up this morning from Tampa Medical Center and transferred here. If she's situated, I'd like to see her."

The girl looked at her computer. "Hmmm. I don't remember anyone coming in. What is the patient's name?"

"Quinn Rogers."

She studied the screen, then looked at him and back at the screen. "We're not scheduled to pick her up until ten a.m.."

Brian took a deep breath. This was it. "I don't understand. Your ambulance arrived at the hospital at eight and took her."

"Hold on." She picked up her phone and turned to whisper into the receiver. She turned back and gave him a forced smile. "The Director of Nursing is on her way down."

Less than a minute later, a woman in scrubs rushed through the door. "Dr. Rogers, I'm Connie. We're not scheduled to pick your daughter up for another hour. Are you sure she's left the hospital?"

Now he let them see how much his hands were shaking. "I left when the ambulance arrived. I stopped at the police station to give you time to get situated."

Connie glanced at the nurse. "Can you get the social worker from the hospital on the line and then get Dottie as well? We need to speak with both of them." She grabbed her phone out of her pocket and pushed a button. "Hey, it's Connie. Can you check the ambulance bay? Let me know which truck is out?"

Brian chewed his thumb. His wife had always said he was a terrible liar. He had to hope he'd gotten better, for Quinn's sake.

"Thank you for checking." She hung up the phone. "All of our ambulances are accounted for. None have left the facility today."

"Connie. The hospital is on the line." The receptionist handed her the phone.

"Hi. This is the Director of Nursing at Healing

Hearts Long Term Care. We have Dr. Rogers here. He says his daughter was picked up by our transport team at eight a.m. but we're not scheduled to get her until ten a.m. Can you confirm if the patient is still there?"

She leaned the receiver away from her face. "They're checking. It'll be just a minute."

Brian nodded and started pacing. The poor receptionist looked ready to cry.

"Yes, I'm still here." She tapped her nails on the desk as she listened. "Can you send us the video clip from the ambulance bay? Our ambulances haven't gone out today."

She listened for a few minutes before hanging up.

"Dr. Rogers. I'm going to put you in the conference room by my office. The hospital is tracking down the ambulance company that picked her up. It's quite possible she was taken to the wrong facility, so we need time to let the hospital investigate."

He sat on the couch in the small meeting room as the receptionist walked in with a bottle of water. Her eyes filled with tears. "If you need anything, I'm right out front."

This poor girl was going to have nightmares after

this. She looked like it was her fault his daughter was missing. He felt bad for her, but he couldn't do anything about it. His focus was on his little girl and giving her the best chance he could.

As time passed, he fixated on the clock. Quinn had been taken two and a half hours ago. The unknown number had texted the package was secured in the new delivery van, but he hadn't heard anything since. A thousand things could be wrong and he was sitting in this room doing nothing. He jumped up and paced the room.

The hospital had given up on her. There was nothing more they could do. Did they really expect him to just watch her die? His plan to save her was ludicrous, but he had to believe he was doing the right thing.

The door opened as Connie let Detective Franklin in.

He paled. He'd been expecting a patrolman. No hope for it now. "What's happening? They picked up my daughter hours ago. Have they found her?" His voice got louder with each word.

Detective Franklin clenched his jaw. "The hospital has confirmed Ms. Rogers has been trans- ferred. The ambulance that picked her up didn't belong to this facility. It was a private transport, and they have confirmed that the truck was stolen this morning."

"Are you fucking kidding me? They lost my daughter? Who just lets a critical patient leave without verifying who took her? How could they let this happen?" By the time he finished, he was out of breath. His chest rising and falling rapidly as he tried to regain composure.

"We have an APB out on the ambulance. We're trying to identify the people in the truck, but their faces were hidden by hats and they kept their heads down. We are doing everything we can to find her."

Connie stepped forward. "You are welcome to wait here as long as you want while we wait for word."

He shook his head. "I can't just sit here. Someone out there has her. I'm going to drive around and look for the ambulance. If you get any more news, please call me right away."

"We'd prefer you go home and let us handle this. We don't know who took her or why and we don't need to worry about you being out on the streets, too."

He shook his head at the detective. "I'm sorry. If it was your daughter, you wouldn't just sit here."

The older man nodded and stepped aside.

Brian tried to walk calmly when all he wanted to do was run to his car and get to the house. Greg was fantastic, but he needed to see for himself that she was okay. He trusted the other man, but when it came down to it, he was a drug addict and who knows how long it's been since his last fix.

He drove in circles for a bit. He doubted the detective had anyone following him but better to be safe than sorry.

After half an hour, he pulled into the two-car garage of the house. The van was empty.

He rushed into the house and to the back bedroom, where he'd had a hospital bed delivered. Greg and Christina were sitting in chairs next to it.

They jumped up when they saw him.

"Is she good?" He rushed over to the bed and checked each machine.

"We had no issue at all. She never woke up, and we were very careful each time we moved her. It took a long time to get her moved to this bed since we don't know exactly where all the burns are. We went really slow, but again, she never moved."

"Good, good." He brushed the hair back from her forehead. "Everything is going as planned so far. The cops are out looking for the ambulance. They said they didn't expect to be able to identify you guys because you hid your faces so well."

"How'd it go at the facility?" Christina asked.

"Connie was very nice and I think I scarred your poor receptionist. She looked devastated for me."

"Aww. Lily is a sweet girl. I'll check on her on my next shift."

"I have some research to do, so I'll sit with her for a while. You can go get something to eat." They nodded and turned to leave, but he stopped them. "If you need a fix, take just enough to take the edge off. I can't have you high when I need you."

Greg rolled his eyes, "Yeah man, we're not stupid. We got it."

Brian watched them leave with a scowl. He had to trust them, but it was so hard when he knew Quinn was going to be in their care when he wasn't around. "I'm sorry baby, I hope that wasn't too rough on you. I'm going to help you, I promise."

He knew she was still under and would stay that way for a while yet, but he still held out hope she'd move or something to let him know she heard him.

He made a mental note to check her IV to see how much Propofol she had left and get more soon. He couldn't let her run out. He grabbed his laptop and logged into the shifter database. That nature show had given him an idea and now he had to put it into action. With any luck, in a few days, his baby girl would be on the mend.

CHAPTER
Twenty-Six

BRIAN WALKED into the hospital vaguely noting the odd looks and whispers that followed him as he punched the button to the elevator to head up to his floor. He was sure part of the reason was he looked like shit. Sleep hadn't been his friend since this all started after all.

As the doors opened, he stepped off and came to an abrupt halt as one of the nurses stopped him to check in. "Dr. Rogers," she exclaimed in surprise. "We didn't expect to see you here. Is there something I can help you with?"

"No, Becky." He replied with an awkward smile. "I left abruptly and had a few things I needed to wrap up. I was going crazy at home, so I thought getting away for a bit might help me."

She patted his shoulder comfortingly and kept going.

He unlocked his office and sat at the desk. He'd give it fifteen minutes, then do what he was really here for.

Someone knocked on his door. Sheila Carpenter, his boss, poked her head in. "Brian. We heard about your daughter. How's everything going?"

"Actually, I'm going kind of insane. My daughter was being transported this morning from the hospital to a facility and the ambulance has disappeared."

She gasped and sat down across from his desk. "Oh my god. How horrible."

He nodded. "The police are looking for her, but they told me to stay off the streets. I can't just sit in my house. I was just stopping in for a minute, then I'll be heading back out. Thank you so much for asking."

"Of course, if there is anything I or we can do, please let us know."

"Thank you. Honestly, I'm not sure what could be done, but thank you for that." Brian glanced around the room awkwardly.

"You know you can take your time and come back when you're ready."

Brian nodded. "If it's okay, I'd like to come back for at least a few hours a day. My hands are tied, and sitting home alone will just make me go insane, you know."

He met Sheila's eye and let the fear and pain fill his eyes for her to see. He needed to be able to get any supplies Greg and Christina couldn't get for him and if she said no, he wasn't sure what he'd do.

Sheila stood up to leave. "I know how empty the house must feel. I don't blame you for wanting to be here. You work when you need to and take off when you want. We'll make sure everything gets covered here."

He waited five minutes before heading out. There was only one tool he hadn't been able to get, so he was going to have to take it from the hospital. Thankfully, it wasn't something the hospital monitored closely, so it shouldn't be missed.

He nodded at people as he made his way through the halls toward the procedure room where sterile trays and trocars were kept. He stood down the hall from the door, pretending to be on his phone. When he was sure the room was empty, he held his breath and badged in. In theory, he had badge access to almost everywhere in the hospital, but he was always waiting for something in the plan to go wrong.

He searched the labeled drawers until he found what he needed. He grabbed a couple of trocars and slid them into his backpack. Now he just had to figure out how to get close to the shifter who was hopefully going to save Quinn's life.

"Greg, I'm going out for a bit. If things go as planned, when I get back, be prepared to do a procedure." Brian grabbed his keys and stared at Greg to make sure he was paying attention. "Are you high, or can you do this?"

"I'm not always on shit, man. Give me some credit." Greg paused and frowned. "What exactly are you going to do, anyway?"

"Don't worry about it yet. Just keep an eye on Quinn." He wanted to throw up. He'd never done a violent thing in his life and he'd never been very athletic. Dads do what they have to do, though.

It was a bit early yet, so he stopped in at the police department and raised hell. He had to keep up appearances, after all.

The deputy at the desk greeted him as he walked

in, and Brian asked for Detective Franklin. Within a few minutes, he was being led back to an office.

"Have a seat, Dr. Rogers. I wish I had better news for you, but rest assured we're doing everything we can to find her." Detective Franklin assured Brian.

"How does something like this happen?" He demanded.

Detective Franklin blew out a breath. "I don't know. We will not give up though, we will find her."

Brian nodded and then stood up. "I sure hope so, because I am not going to go away. I'll be here every day checking in and making sure you're doing your job."

"I understand." Detective Franklin escorted Brian to the front of the building. "I'll see you tomorrow and, with luck, we'll have some news."

Brian left the precinct and climbed into his car. He laid his head on the steering wheel and blew out a breath of relief that he'd pulled that off.

His phone rang startling him. "What's wrong?"

"Quinn is fine, or well still the same at least. But we accidentally set the alarm off." Greg quickly explained. "We put the code in, but the alarm went off."

Greg cursed, "I'll take care of it. Just be more

careful next time." He hung up and then dialed his old friend.

"Hello?"

"Hey Fred, It's Brian Rogers. In case you get a call about the alarm going off, that was me. I got a leak in my apartment, so I borrowed your place. Hope that's okay."

Dr. Hamlin laughed, "No worries. I gave you the free use of the place when you wanted. Stay as long as you need."

They talked for a few more minutes, before saying goodbye and hanging up. Brian blew out a breath in relief. The last thing he wanted right now was a stupid complication like an alarm to ruin everything they were doing.

He drove to the house he had scoped out the night before. The salamander shifter who lived there had gone for a jog in the park by his house. Brian was banking on it being a routine. He went into the park and sat on a bench. When he saw the shifter coming, he stood and pretended to stretch his legs. He pulled the syringe of Propofol out of his jacket pocket and got ready. After he was a few steps past Brian, he rushed up behind him and stuck the needle in his neck, pushing the medicine in as fast as he could.

It was a large dose, but everything he'd read said paranormals metabolized medications and alcohol much faster than humans.

The shifter stumbled a few feet and went down. Brian grabbed him under the arms and dragged him into the bushes. He bent over the man, out of breath as he watched him go completely unconscious. "I'm very sorry, but you are doing a good thing."

He unzipped the pouch strapped to his back and took out the alcohol wipes. He rolled the shifter onto his side and pulled his pants down enough to expose his hip. The alcohol wipe burned his nose as he cleaned the area. He grabbed the syringe of lidocaine and numbed the area before he pushed the trocar in. When he felt it hit the bone he twisted. As a medical examiner he'd been steadfast, but being in the bushes, stealing bone marrow and stem cells from an unconscious person had his hands shaking. After he drew the fluids from the bone, he pulled the trocar out and noticed the tip was broken off. His need to be fast had made him sloppy. He grabbed the second trocar and repeated the process on the other hip. Five minutes had already passed, and he still had to draw blood.

When he had everything he needed, he packed

up quickly and thanked the unconscious man again for his help.

He jogged to the car and flopped into the driver's seat. Laughter erupted from him. Now that the adrenaline was wearing off he felt utter relief that he'd managed to pull it off.

Greg and Christina were sitting at the kitchen table eating spaghetti. Brian held up his bag. "I'll be in with Quinn, fingers crossed this works."

"While you were gone, we gave her morphine and changed her bandages." Christina said before shoving a big bite into her mouth. "Her blood pressure went up a bit, but it's stable now."

Brian went in to check on Quinn. She didn't look any better or worse. "Hang in there, sweetheart. Daddy has the magic cure. At least I hope I do." He blew out a breath and sat beside her. "If this works, it'll help you heal faster."

Greg walked in and leaned against the wall. "What exactly are you doing, anyway?"

"I'm going to give her some salamander stem cells that should help her heal."

"Do I want to know where you got that from?" Greg arched an eyebrow and moved to stand beside him. "That's not something I can even get my hands on."

Brian shrugged. "Don't ask questions you don't want the answers to."

He sterilized the trocar and pulled some of Quinn's bone marrow. He mixed the salamanders and Quinn's together to help reduce the chance of a reaction. The IV infusion would take anywhere from fifteen minutes to a couple of hours. Then the waiting would begin as he watched her closely for any complications. As he kissed her brow, he noted she was cool to the touch.

"Brian." Christina shook his shoulder. "Why don't you go lay down. It's been four hours and so far no negative reaction. I'll sit in here and keep an eye on her while you get some sleep. I can't imagine you've had much since the accident."

He blinked the sleep away. "I can't believe I fell asleep." He checked all the monitors to reassure himself that she was fine. This procedure was unheard of, so he really had no idea what to expect.

He yawned deeply. "If you're sure you're good, I'd love to lay down in a real bed for a couple of hours."

She stepped back to let him move past. "Sounds good and I promise if anything changes, I will come get you immediately."

Brian woke up with a start as he saw the light coming in from the window. He'd slept far longer than he'd planned. He jumped out of the bed and raced down the hall, skidding to a stop outside her door.

"Why didn't you wake me up?"

Greg smiled, "Because she's doing great and you needed the sleep."

Brian tentatively stepped into the room as he saw Quinn's fingers twitching for the first time. "Did you see that?" He cried out as he pointed to her hand as tears fell down his face. "She moved."

Christina nodded. "She started doing that a couple of hours ago. It's a good sign, right?"

"Yes, it is." Brian moved closer and peeled the edge of one of the bandages slowly just in case. He hoped that the salamander's stem cells had healed her burns, but he couldn't be sure it worked like that until he looked.

He fell to his knees, sobbing as he laid his head on the edge of the bed. "It fucking worked, look." He cried in happiness.

"What did?" Greg asked as he stood up and moved closer to the bed. "What's going on? I don't understand."

Brian jumped up and pulled off one of the

bandages to show her unburned skin. "Look, it's healing."

Christina gasped as she gently reached out and pulled back another bandage to reveal slightly pink skin. "Holy shit."

Brian nodded as he leaned down close to Quinn's ear to talk to her. "It's working, Quinn. I told you this would work. You're healing, baby girl. I'm so proud of you. Before you know it, you'll be opening those beautiful eyes of yours."

Greg cocked his head. "The salamander's stem cells did that?"

"Yes." Brian sat down in a chair and stared at Quinn. "With luck, we'll see even more progress as the day goes on. This could be the turning point we needed."

"Look at her hands." Christina whispered in awe. "They have color again. She's not so pale."

Brian grinned as he stood up and pulled down Quinn's bottom lip to see the inside. It was one of the easiest ways to tell if someone was anemic. Her's had been white, but now it was beautiful pink. The stem cells had reversed the anemia.

A few hours later, he stared at the monitor, frustrated. The stem cells had worked beautifully on her burns, but so far, her liver, lungs, and kidneys hadn't improved. If they didn't turn around soon, she was going to go into total organ failure.

He stood up excitedly and rushed for his laptop. If the stem cells worked this well, what else could the shifters do to heal the rest of her? Was there something he could give her that would make her invincible to being hurt? If he could make her impossibly strong, he'd never have to worry about her again.

"Brian." Greg called, interrupting his research.

"What?" He asked as he came back into Quinn's room and smiled at the pink tinge to his baby girl's cheeks.

"Look at her urine output." Greg pointed. "Her output has decreased to less than five cc's an hour. At this rate, she will not be able to survive much longer."

"No, goddamn it. It's one step forward and two steps back. We've not come this far to lose her now. I've got to run to the hospital for a few hours to pick up some supplies. Let me know if there's any change immediately."

"You got it, sugar. I'll be here for a while, then I have to go to work. But Greg will be here if you're not back by then. Don't worry, we've got her." Christina reassured him with a soft smile.

But first he had to make his daily stop by the police station to harass Detective Franklin for any news and demand answers.

Brian entered his office and dropped the duffle bag he'd been carrying on one of the chairs in front of the desk. He moved to sit in his chair so he could have a minute to think. He had a list of things he needed to get, and now he had to plan how to do it without getting caught. At the top of the list was a ventilator. The portable one Quinn had was great, but it wasn't going to last forever and he wanted one on hand now, so he didn't have to worry.

Over the next few hours, he randomly went from area to area and took the items he needed. Now that he'd taken the vent, anti-rejection meds, and Propofol, among other things, it was just a matter of time before the various departments realized their inventories were off. It would take the hospital a bit longer to do a full rundown. Then his access to supplies would be limited to whatever Greg and Christina could get.

He tried to look calm as he left the hospital. If

anyone asked to look in his bag, he'd have no explanation.

The walk to his car felt miles long. Always ready for someone to come tackle him.

He made it home and carried the supplies in, setting them up on the kitchen table. Greg and Christina looked through the items.

Greg whistled. "I think you've been keeping some stuff from us. This is way more than monitoring a patient."

Brian tried to brush it off. "It's not a big deal. You guys are doing great. Just stick with me a bit longer." He pushed past them and went to check on Quinn.

Christina came in with a bucket of water and towels. "Since her burns are pretty much healed, I thought I'd give her a proper sponge bath. Greg is making dinner."

"Thank you for this. I know it's an unusual situation, but you guys are being awesome."

"Well, you are paying us. But we did go into medicine for a reason, and your daughter didn't deserve any of this."

He nodded as he walked to the door. "I've got some research to do on my laptop, so I'll leave you to it."

He needed to pick the next shifter. It was their

fault they were in this situation, so shouldn't they be the ones to save her?

Brian sat in his car just down the street from the wolf shifter and observed him. He'd gotten as much information online as he could, but since he was only adequate with a computer, it wasn't much. After a few hours of waiting and nothing happening, he called Greg and told him to meet him to get rid of the ambulance.

It was close to two in the morning, so the streets would be empty, making it less likely they'd be seen. He'd planned for this, so he had gas cans in the truck all ready to go. He took one last look at the quiet complex and pulled out. From where he was, it'd take about half an hour to reach his destination and the empty area he'd picked to burn the vehicle.

He pulled up a couple of seconds after Greg had arrived. The other man climbed out of the ambulance with an attitude, yelling at Brian, which pissed him off until they both got in each other's face screaming.

"What the fuck is your problem?" Brian demanded.

"You're not telling us everything. You left your computer logged in and I snooped. Why are you on the shifter database? What in the hell are you planning?"

"Does it matter? You're being paid really well." Brian shot back.

"Some stem cells are one thing, but come on. Between the stuff you brought back from the hospital and the list you had up on your laptop, I'm not sure Christina and I want to get any deeper into whatever this is."

Brian scoffed and turned back to his car. He popped the trunk and pulled out the gas cans. "Here, help me douse the damn thing so we can get out of here."

It only took them a few minutes to cover the ambulance inside and out in gasoline and then to set it ablaze. They watched for a minute to make sure it was fully engulfed before placing the cans back in the trunk and leaving. Everything was going perfectly.

CHAPTER
Twenty~Seven

BRIAN WAS REALLY DOING THIS. As much as he didn't want to harm another person, it was the only way. The werewolf shifter walked out of his apartment building at the same he had the morning before.

Brian grabbed the syringe of Propofol out of his jacket pocket and followed behind him. He was an easy mark because very few people were out at four-thirty in the morning, but according to his file, he was a garbage man, so his day was starting soon.

As they were coming up on an alleyway, Brian rushed forward and injected him. This was a massive dose compared to the one he'd given the salamander. He needed him alive just long enough to get what he needed, then he'd let the Propofol take him the rest of the way.

The werewolf roared and looked like he was trying to shift, but the medicine overtook him and he dropped.

Brian glanced around and didn't see anyone. He dragged the man into the alleyway behind a large stack of boxes so they were hidden from view of the road.

He kneeled next to him and got close to his ear. "I'm so sorry. I don't want to do this, but you are doing a good thing."

He dropped his backpack to the ground beside him and pulled out some gloves and pulled them on. With a hat to keep his hair out of his eyes, he was as ready as he was going to get. To keep the werewolf from shouting again, he numbed his side with the novocaine he'd gotten from the ambulance. He cut a seven-inch incision on the side of his abdomen and cut through layers of tissue and muscle before carefully removing the kidney, ureter, and blood vessels. He then placed the organs in a small cooler and started on the other side.

He packed everything back into his backpack, then checked the man's pulse. He was gone.

His hands shook as he drove to the house. He'd

done it. He'd killed someone. He couldn't even feel remorse. It was worth it. Quinn was worth all of it.

He rushed into the house and straight to the room Greg and Christina were sharing. He knocked loudly and called the other man's name.

Greg stumbled to the door, yawning loudly. "What's wrong?"

"It's time for a procedure." He held up the cooler, then turned and left for Quinn's room.

"Is that blood on your clothes?" He called out as he pulled a shirt on.

Brian ignored him as he entered the room and nudged Christina. "We need to do a procedure. Can you put on some coffee while we prep? Then I could use your help."

She nodded and went to the kitchen.

He set the cooler on the dresser and pulled his bloody shirt off and tossed it in the garbage.

Greg opened the cooler and looked inside. "Oh, my fucking god. What did you do?"

"It's too late for you to worry about it now. Let's not waste anyone's donation."

"Somehow, I don't think this was a donation. That implies it was willingly given." Greg snapped.

Brian stopped and dropped his head forward. "I'm going to burn in hell for what I'm doing, but I'm okay with that if it means Quinn gets to live a long life. When this is all over, I'll process everything that's happening. For now, I just need to keep moving forward."

There would be time to atone for his sins later. "Let's get washed up."

As they were gloving up, Christina returned with three mugs. She glanced in the cooler, then at Greg.

Brian didn't have time to convince her. What was done was done. Now it was time to save his daughter. "Okay, let's get started. Greg, I need her completely under and know she can handle the anesthesia. It will take a while to attach the blood vessels, ureters, and kidneys. If you notice any fluctuations in her vital signs, let me know right away." He made a clean cut on her left side, removed her kidney, and implanted the werewolf's. It was larger, but wouldn't be an issue. Christina scrambled to hang fluids to keep the blood pressure up and hand instruments to Brian.

He nodded his thanks. "I need you to prepare the next kidney so we can close as soon as possible."

"I think she's stable and handling the transplant with minimal medication support," Greg said.

Brian pulled the bloody gloves off and tossed them in a medical waste bag he'd taken from the hospital. "She was under anesthesia for a little over five hours, so we'll watch for her to show signs of movement. We should begin to see urine output within the next hour or so."

Greg stood up and stretched. "It's been a while since I've had to sit still for so long."

Brian walked over and studied the monitor. "Christina, watch for any signs of bleeding and let me know right away if you see anything. We need to start her on anti-rejection medications and start giving her the Brompton Solution for pain. If she starts fidgeting or her blood pressure rises, give her more." He paused and studied Quinn. "I took these from a werewolf shifter so we really have no idea what to expect."

Greg spun around and glared at him. "Are you fucking kidding me? You killed a shifter? Are you crazy?"

Christina paced back and forth, ringing her hands. "I don't know about this. It was all a bit crazy to start, but now we're involving shifters."

Brian rolled his eyes. "Humans can't save her. She needed more. She needed magic, and shifters are magic. Look what the salamander stem cells did. These kidneys should be ten times better than the regular human pair she had." He shrugged. "That's my theory, at least."

Greg shook his head. "You're fucking crazy." He stormed out of the room.

Brian reached over and gently touched Christina's hand. "We're too far gone now. Please help me save her."

Christina stared at Quinn for a few seconds before nodding. "She didn't deserve any of this. I'm not going anywhere, I promise."

Brian was exhausted. He'd been up almost thirty-six hours sitting by her bed watching for signs the kidney transplant had been successful. It'd been twenty-four hours since they closed her up and the surgery appeared to have worked. She still had a long way to go and more organs to fix, but at least he could take kidneys off the list.

Greg walked into the room and handed him a salad. "You need to eat. I'll sit with her for a while."

Brian took the food gratefully. "I think it's time to reach out to your blood guy. We're going to need some on hand."

Greg pulled his phone out of his pocket. "I'll set up a meeting and text you an address and time."

Brian's eyes bulged. "You want me to go meet a vampire?"

"If you are willing to kill paranormals and steal their organs, you can handle meeting a vampire. Just leave him alive. I need him."

Brian stormed out of the room. Judgmental asshole.

He showered and left for the police station. He had to maintain his cover story.

The patrolman at the desk nodded at him. Stopping by four days out of six tends to leave an impression. "I'll let Detective Franklin know you're here."

A few minutes later, the door opened, and the detective led him to the usual conference room. "So, what's the latest on my daughter?"

The other man sat down with a sigh. "I wish I had better news for you, but we don't have an update. We're still looking for the ambulance. I assume you still haven't heard anything from the kidnappers?"

Brian shook his head. "No phone calls, nothing. I'm not home much. I've been spending some time at the hospital to keep busy and the rest of the time I'm out driving around, hoping to find her or the ambulance. I still don't understand why someone would want to take her?"

Detective Franklin tapped his fingers on the table. "We still have a lot of avenues to pursue."

Brian slammed his hand on the table. "What about the monsters that did this? Maybe they took her to finish off the job?"

The other man looked sad for him. "That's not likely, since none of the other victims have been taken."

Brian laid his hands on his head. He'd be so glad when he didn't have to do this anymore. He cleared his throat and stood up. "Thank you for your time. I hope to hear good news soon."

He made his way out of the station to the hospital. He was going to need more supplies for the next procedure and time was against him. Any day now, they should figure out a ventilator was missing from maintenance and when that happened, they'd start looking for other missing items.

The usual sad smiles greeted him as he made his way to his office to work for a bit. When enough time had passed, he pulled out the duffel bag he'd left the last time he was in and went for supplies. Between the rib spreader, the bone saw, and the ECMO machine, he was going to have to be very smart about where he took them from.

As he was placing the last supply into the bag, his phone buzzed. It was a text from Greg to meet the vampire in thirty minutes.

GPS showed it would take almost that long to drive to the meeting place. He still couldn't believe he was going to talk to a vampire. He didn't even recognize himself any longer.

The paranormal bar was quiet in the middle of the day. As instructed, he made his way around the back and knocked.

A thin, pale man in his twenties answered. "Yeah?"

Brian gulped. "Greg sent me to pick up a package."

The vampire swung the door open. "Follow me."

The bar was nearly pitch black. He glanced in a room and saw several people on beds hooked up to machines that looked like they were donating blood.

They passed the main bar area. A woman was sitting in a booth feeding on a man.

He had no idea places like this existed. Although it made sense. Better to do it here where it's monitored and not take it from an unwilling human.

The man took him to a room full of fridges.

"Greg didn't say how much you need. It's two fifty per bag for human blood and four hundred for vamp blood. If you haven't tasted our blood before, be prepared for the high of your life. Make sure you're in a safe place the first time you use it."

His mind immediately ran through the possibilities. What could the vamp blood do for Quinn. Would it be as useful as the salamander stem cells were? Brian grabbed his wallet out of his back pocket. "I'll take four of the vamp."

The vampire took the cash and put the four bags in a small cooler. "If you need more, you know where to find me."

Brian's hands shook the entire way out. It's not like one of them were going to pounce on him and drain him, but this was also the closest he had ever been to any of their kind.

Now to scout out his next donor.

CHAPTER
Twenty-Eight

BRIAN WATCHED the mermaid splashing in the bay. Every few minutes, she would dive out and cut a fisherman's line from the pier above. If he wasn't so nervous, he'd find it funny.

When she came back to the shore, he did his best fake laugh and walked toward her, carrying a large backpack. "That is great. Are you sabotaging their lines?"

The woman looked at him wearily. "I'm just protecting my aquatic friends."

"I can't believe none of them know it's you doing it." He tried to look properly impressed.

She snorted. "There have been plenty of angry men coming at me. I'm not afraid, though."

Brian's eyes got wide. "Um, I think one of those

fishermen is coming this way." He pointed behind her. When she turned, he stuck the needle in her neck and caught her on her way down.

He dragged her to the firmest part of the sand and laid her down. She moaned quietly as her eyes rolled back in her head.

"Take faith that you're doing a good thing. Quinn will be eternally grateful."

The injection of Propofol was a toxic dose, so she wouldn't feel any pain. He pulled the backpack from his shoulder and pulled out the scalpel, rib spreader and saw. He pulled his phone out and opened his music app to play rock music as loud as possible.

He splashed antiseptic on her chest area. The incision was long and exposed the sternum. He applied the rib spreader with slow turns after cutting open the cavity. The ice cooler was open and ready for the lungs as he removed them with swift precision. The seawater from her body transferred with the organs as he put them in the cooler, but that couldn't be helped. He could clean them properly when he got home. Sweat ran down his back as he rushed to pack up everything and get out of there. Hopefully, by leaving her in the open, they'd find her quickly. She didn't deserve to stay down there long.

He drove home in a daze. His oath to do no harm

was obliterated now. He grabbed his phone and texted Greg to get the ECMO machine he'd stolen the day before setup and blood on hand.

Christina stood in the door to Quinn's room, watching for him to arrive. She was already gloved up. He handed her the cooler. "Can you clean these well while I get cleaned up?"

She nodded hesitantly and went into the room. He changed out of his bloody, sandy clothes and washed as fast as possible.

When he entered the room, he didn't make eye contact with Greg. He could imagine the death stare the man was giving him.

He gloved up and checked the kidney incisions from two days earlier. "These are healing so fast. It really is insane how quickly shifters heal."

Greg moved to Quinn's head and started the anesthesia.

"Settle in. This is going to take a bit longer than the kidneys did." Brian took a deep breath and made the first incision. He did his best to not look up at her face. It was easier to pretend it was some random patient from his days during residency. He inserted the tubing into the blood vessels to set the ECMO machine up and be ready to take over her blood circulation during the lung removal. The sound of the saw slicing through the sternum was chilling, but nothing prepared him for the sight of just how damaged her lungs were.

The fragile tissue was harder to remove, and blood pooled in the cavity. The mermaid's lungs were larger, which complicated things. Brian growled in frustration as he fought to attach the airway. The longer he took, the more blood she was losing.

"Greg, get two units of blood up and infused as soon as you can," He demanded. His hands shook as he started the closure while he prayed this would take. "Christina, make sure the blood is infused over the next two hours and we'll keep her fluids running for the next twelve hours."

He grabbed his phone and collapsed into the chair. There was a phone call and a voicemail from Detective Franklin. He pushed the button and played it on speaker.

"Hi Dr. Rogers. We've decided to hold a press conference tomorrow at eleven a.m. to see if the public can help. We would love it if you'd be there, but understand if you'd rather not."

Christina cracked open a can of beer and sat across from him. "So you gonna go?"

"It saves time from me having to make an

appearance and it makes me look like a grieving father."

Greg pulled a chair in and sat next to Christina. For a few minutes, everyone was silent. The only sounds in the room were the ventilator and the beeps from the oxygen monitor.

Greg crossed his ankles as he stretched out. "I can't believe this has worked so far. She is a medical miracle for even surviving the procedures. She might just be able to pull through this."

Brian nodded. "Infection is still a huge risk. Especially with the sand and sea water we had to deal with. Not to mention we have no idea what this is doing to her latent paranormal gene."

Christina drew her eyebrows together. "She has a latent gene?"

"All of us do. Every single human. We don't know why they're latent. Why our world is different from theirs. What made us all human and them all paranormal."

Christina stared at her hands. "So I could turn into a supe?"

Greg shook his head. "I've never heard of a human turning. I think you're safe."

"There was that cop a couple of months ago. It was all anyone talked about at the hospital for weeks. The guy was attacked and died, then came back to life and is now some kind of shifter."

Christina's smile got big. "I think it would be kind of cool to change. I want to fly, or maybe breathe fire. There are so many cool things they can do."

Brian shrugged. "What's that saying, with great power comes great responsibility. Because those two fought, my baby is laying here fighting for her life. Now they get to save it too."

CHAPTER
Twenty-Nine

"BRIAN, wake up. You have to see this." Christina was leaning close to Quinn, staring at her.

He jumped out of his chair, rubbing the sleep from his eyes. "What happened?"

She pointed at Quinn's neck.

Brian leaned down and blinked several times. He couldn't possibly be seeing what he thought he saw. "Are those... are those..."

Greg walked in, sipping his coffee. "What's happening?"

Christina stepped back to let him get close.

"Holy shit. Are those gills?" Greg reached up and poked them, making them flutter. "Oh, that's kind of disgusting."

Brian shook his head. "There is nothing

disgusting about this. It's a beautiful miracle. I wanted the mermaid lungs to give her the strongest lungs in the world. With these gills, she'll be impervious to drowning now too. It's accidentally perfect."

Hours later, Christina stood up and moved closer to the monitor. Brian watched her and saw what she was looking at. Quinn was breathing above the vent and causing the alarms to trigger. Even with the sedation which she needed for the pain, her lungs were already functioning so well she would need to come off the vent.

"Greg," Brian called out. Greg nodded and quickly lowered the vent settings. The lungs were far superior to her human ones.

"I'm going to remove the tube and place her on oxygen via a nasal cannula."

Brian acknowledged him as he stepped back to study Quinn. What else could he give her that would make it so she would always be safe and have the best chance of survival? With the lungs and gills, she could hold her breath and swim under water without fear of drowning. The salamander cells gave her regeneration and healing abilities. His mind switched back to the shifter database and the different paranormals he'd seen listed. Wings? What if he gave her wings so she could fly from any situation? He raced out of the room and back to his computer to find a suitable donor.

His phone buzzed in his pocket a short time later. The calendar reminder to get to the police station was blinking at him. He headed back into Quinn's room. "Can you guys keep an eye on her for any more changes while I go to the press conference?"

Greg was still staring at the gills. "I'm not going anywhere. This is fascinating. I'm wondering if she's going to turn into a werewolf on the next full moon."

As Brian left, he heard Christina respond. "Is that really a thing? I thought that was a myth."

Brian chuckled as he made his way to his car. He had no idea what adding all these paranormal organs was going to do for her, but she was still alive, so he was taking it as a blessing for now.

"Good morning. I'm Chief Henry Barlowe with the Tampa PD. On February tenth, one of the victims from the downtown attack was being transported from the hospital to a private facility. Two unknown perpetrators stole an ambulance and kidnapped her, pretending to be the transport team from the facility.

The patient is eighteen-year-old Quinn Rogers. Her father, Dr. Brian Rogers, is here with us today." Brian waved to the cameras awkwardly. "Ms. Rogers is critically injured still. Few people would be able to take care of her medical needs. We need the public's help to find Ms. Rogers or the ambulance. We'll be releasing pictures of the vehicle and the two suspects and opening a tip line. It is vital that you think back to that day and if there is even the smallest thing that might be related, call it in. Let us decide if it's important. We need to make sure Ms. Rogers is okay and reunite her with her father. I'll take a few questions."

Brian's hands were fisted in his pockets. This was a nightmare. He was duping so many people. He had to keep reminding himself that this was for Quinn, all of it was for her and her future.

CHAPTER
Thirty

BRIAN SAT behind the air conditioner unit, waiting for the next shifter. Even in the early morning hours, wearing the jumpsuit to protect his clothes was making him sweat. To pass the time, he thought back to the day before. After the press conference, he'd scouted the building and knew the gargoyle flew to and from work, using the roof for access. It hadn't taken but a few minutes to establish the lack of security in the building.

He didn't know what time the man was going to appear, so he'd been sitting up there since five a.m..

The nerves of waiting for him were taking its toll. The longer he sat there, the closer he was to chickening out.

Finally, off in the distance, the winged creature

came into view and swiftly landed on the roof. Brian watched as the man came to a stop. In order to get the wings, he was going to have to knock him out before he shifted back to human. With their rapid healing powers, it was going to take a massive dose of Propofol.

The gargoyle folded its wings in and bent down to grab a duffle bag out of a locked cabinet.

Brian grabbed the syringe out of his pocket and rushed the monster. He jumped on its back and held on while he used every ounce of strength to get the needle to pierce the skin. Within seconds, the gargoyle was face down on the roof. Once in a while he'd twitch, but otherwise was silent. The man would be grateful later that Brian wasn't killing him. He didn't need to, since he was taking an external part of him.

Brian grabbed the scalpel and lifted the right wing. The man gasped quickly several times, then went still. He tossed the scalpel down and checked the creature's neck. When he didn't find a pulse, he went up to his nose. With his skin so thick, maybe Brian just couldn't feel it. After a few seconds with no breath, he sat back on his ass. "I'm sorry. I didn't want to kill you. There's no handbook on dosages for supernatural creatures." He knew the man couldn't hear him, but it still made him feel a little better to apologize.

He picked the scalpel back up and made the first incision. He looked up at the gargoyle's face to make sure he really was dead. There was no movement, not even a twitch.

He tried gliding the scalpel down to widen the incision and realized the skin was way thicker than he expected. His arms shook as he used two hands to make the cuts. They were jagged, but he'd have to hope Quinn's new stem cells would heal the incisions well enough no one would see the scars.

One after the other, he managed to get the wings off. He was exhausted, but still had hours to go. He groaned as he folded them as small as possible and shoved them in the duffle bag. He had to sit on it to compress it enough for him to zip it closed.

He glanced at his phone and saw it was almost eight o'clock. He took the jumpsuit off and balled it up. No one in the building should be able to see a drop of blood on him. He texted Greg to be ready for another procedure and made his way downstairs.

On the drive home, he felt lighter than he had in days. Between the gills and the wings, his girl was going to be the strongest person on Earth. She'd never be hurt again.

Greg and Christina were already prepped and standing next to Quinn.

Brian hefted the large duffle onto the dresser.

Greg looked weary. "What horrors are in store for us today?"

Brian beamed at them. "We're going to have to flip her over." One by one, he pulled out the wings and laid them out on top of the small table they'd dragged in when they first got there.

"Fucking Hell." Greg muttered.

Christina walked over and ran her hand across one of them. "They're incredible. Do you think she'll be able to tuck them into her body the way shifters do, or they'll stay out all the time?"

Brian shrugged. "This is all new territory. Obviously I want her to be able to blend in with the human world, so I hope they disappear inside her, but only time will tell."

Greg sat down at Quinn's head and grabbed the oxygen mask. "I'm going to put her under."

Christina got into position and waited. "So, you have a plan?"

Brian gloved up, opened a surgical kit, and grabbed a scalpel. "I'm going to make the incision and cut down to the muscle to form a pocket and attach the wing, then do the same on the other side.

I'm hoping by connecting them inside instead of just at the skin level, she will be able to control taking them in and out."

Two hours later, he sat back and surveyed the surgery site. The wings had settled in the pocket and he'd sutured the wing base in place. He could already see the skin around the incision getting pink, showing she had good blood flow. Brian stretched his back to loosen the tight muscles. He hadn't expected how hard it would be to close the incision with the tough gargoyle skin.

Christina bent close. "Holy shit. The skin is already scabbing over."

Brian sighed. "I'm worried about the rapid healing of the incision. Will the wings be able to go into her back?"

Greg injected more medicine in her IV. "When this is all over, you really need to write a book about it. You're doing ground-breaking work here. As horrifying as it has been, it's truly miraculous."

Brian tossed his gloves into the bin. "I'm going to do my daily call to the police. We'll know in the next few hours if our luck is holding out.

CHAPTER
Thirty-One

BRIAN YAWNED LOUDLY as he pushed back from the dinner table. "I'm going to sleep for a couple of hours before I relieve Christina."

Christina yelled out to Brian, "Come here quick. I think Quinn is developing early stage sepsis. Her pulse is thready, her temperature is climbing to a hundred point five and her respirations are twenty-six."

Brian nodded as he stopped beside the door. "It stands to reason with the amount of surgeries she has gone through, not to mention the trauma from the accident. I'll have Greg come in and give her some antibiotics. Can you stay with her and monitor her? We need to watch for jaundice and increased fever."

Brian was exhausted, but with the way things were going, his baby girl was going to need a liver. One strong enough to work with the other shifter organs. There weren't many supes he could think of that would fit the bill. Her best chance would be with a phoenix, even though they were extremely rare. He had to hope there were a couple locally and that one of them would be a good candidate.

He blew out a breath. There were only two in the Tampa Bay area.

Greg walked up and glanced over his shoulder. "You don't want to take the guy. He's an agent. The shit they would do to you when they caught you. I'd go with the nurse. Her file says she's single."

Brian glanced up at him. "You seem more accepting of all this now."

Greg shrugged. "Like you said, we're going to burn in hell for this, so might as well make sure your daughter survives it."

"Up to now, I've had at least a day to follow the person and see their routine. I don't think Quinn is going to have that much time. I have a feeling she's going to need a liver as soon as possible. It's almost ten p.m. She's likely in her house until morning."

"Go on social media. People don't realize how much they accidentally give away with their posts."

Brian glanced at the computer, then back at Greg. "Which social media?'

Greg rolled his eyes and plopped into the chair next to him. He opened Facebook and used Brian's saved credentials to log in. He scanned the report from the shifter database, then searched for her name. Lucky for them, her medical file had her picture, so it only took a couple of profiles to find the right one.

"See?" Greg pointed to the screen. "She's got her job listed in her about section. She's a nurse at Bay Area Surgery Center. There are pictures of her with co-workers and some with friends and family, but I don't see a boyfriend or girlfriend. If you're lucky, that means she lives alone. Most surgery center staff go in around five a.m. so your window is pretty small to catch her at home before she leaves."

Brian stared at the pictures on her profile. "Why did you have to look at these? I don't need you to humanize them for me. I need to stay detached so I can get through this." He swallowed past the lump in his throat. Was it too late to switch and take the agent instead?

Brian dressed in dark clothes and made his way to the woman's house. Sunrise wasn't until seven, so he should be able to get close to her house pretty easily.

He parked a few houses away and made his way to a large patch of bushes on her property line. At three thirty, the lights in her house went on. He could go in and surprise her while she was getting ready, but he knew absolutely nothing about breaking and entering. He'd never picked a lock in his life.

He crept closer to the house and crouched behind the large porch swing. His knees were screaming, but he sat patiently with the syringe in his hand.

Finally, he heard steps coming toward the front door. As soon as it opened, he rushed at her and pushed her inside. She got out a small squeak before the Propofol took her down. He dragged her out of view of the front door and kneeled next to her. "You didn't deserve this. I'll find a way to honor all of you when this is over."

Brian made a large midline incision on her abdomen. He carefully dissected the blood vessels and bile duct. He rushed to remove the liver and then placed it in the cooler filled with saline.

He tried to step around the blood to avoid getting any footprints in the puddle. This was by far the messiest and most rushed procedure he'd done so far. He rolled up the jumpsuit he was wearing and shoved it in the backpack. Before he left, he gave her a sad look.

He tried to walk as slow as possible back to the car to not seem out of place. He texted Greg he was on the way with a liver.

When he got home, it was almost four-thirty in the morning. He rushed into the bedroom and put the cooler on the dresser. "How is she?"

Christina pointed at the paper where they'd been charting Quinn's progress since she got there. "She's burning up with a fever. Her urine is a dark amber/brown and is showing more signs of liver failure. She's reaching a critical point and we need to do something soon."

Brian grabbed a pair of gloves out of a box on the table. "I have a liver ready to go. Greg, can you put her under while we get everything set up?"

Greg nodded and went to his place at Quinn's head while Brian and Christina rushed around to lay out the surgical kits and tools.

Brian glanced at Greg. "She ready?"

Greg gave him a thumbs up.

Brian nodded and took a second to stretch his neck from side to side. He splashed antiseptic on her skin and hastily made an incision. Time was against them and he had to hurry.

"Greg, she's going to need at least two units of blood. Can you start them now?" He waited for the other man to nod and start hanging the bags before he continued.

It was a complicated procedure. He removed the diseased liver and implanted the shifter liver quickly. By the fourth hour, he was ready to attach the blood vessels and bile duct. His back screamed when he shifted from one foot to the other. He still had hours to go. Stitching the area had to be meticulous, and he hadn't done this specific procedure since med school.

"Her heart rate is coming down nicely, and she is tolerating the anesthesia." Greg called out.

Brian nodded. "I think her temperature is reacting to the shifter liver and vampire blood, so that is to be expected."

When he was finally done, he closed her up. "Now we wait and see."

Brian yawned as he entered the room where they were keeping Quinn. "What's the latest update?"

"As of three pm, her urine output is normal, and the color is clear. Her temperature is running between ninety-nine and a hundred. The jaundice is clearing as well."

Brian walked up and squeezed Quinn's hand. "Greg, I'm concerned with the amount of medication, sedation, and surgery she has gone through. We need to wake her to assess her neurological status."

Greg nodded as he reached up and turned off the IV Propofol drip. He pulled her eyelids up and flashed a light. "Her pupils are reacting."

Brian let out a relieved sigh. "Okay. Let's see how long it takes her to wake up."

They moved chairs around the bed and sat down.

Brian stared at his phone. It had been half an hour with no change. "This is so frustrating."

Christina patted his back. "Hang in there."

A few minutes later, the blanket over Quinn's legs shifted slightly. "Did you see that?" Brian leaned forward in his seat.

His eyes burned as he stared at the spot. He was afraid to blink and miss another movement.

The heart monitor above her screamed in the silent room. "Her heart rate is one twenty. She's definitely waking up." Greg said unhelpfully. He pushed the button to silence the alarm.

Brian leaned over her so he hovered above her face. "Quinn, honey, can you hear me?" He heard a small moan. "If you can hear me, can you squeeze my hand.?" He grabbed hers and waited.

"Her heart rate just jumped to one forty." Greg called out.

"You need to relax, honey. Try to calm yourself." Brian said softly.

Her eyes flew open as she thrashed around. Her breath came out in rapid pants and she began to sweat.

Christina walked to the other side of the bed and gently brushed the hair away from Quinn's face. "I think she's in a lot of pain and unaware of what has happened. She isn't able to cope with all this pain and she is extremely anxious."

Brian cursed. "I don't understand. Every surgery we've done is nearly healed. She physically looks near perfect. Where is the pain?"

"The only things I can think of is that she is experiencing muscle atrophy, lactic acid buildup, and psychosis from her long trauma. Her body is reacting to some internal turmoil."

Everyone jumped as Quinn let out an ear-piercing scream. Tears poured down Brian's face. The pain etched across her face would be seared into his memory forever. "This is too much. We need to stop this. Push the Brompton's solution. Calm her down."

Greg rushed to inject the pain medicine into her NG tube. Within seconds, Quinn's heart rate started coming down. "Quinn, honey. Is that better?"

Her eyes fluttered closed, and she went still again.

The trio collapsed into their chairs. "Let's let her sleep through the night."

The next afternoon, Brian walked in with a bag of food. "It's Taco Tuesday, so I brought home food for dinner tonight."

"Awesome. How was the hospital? Any indication they are on to you?"

Brian leaned down and kissed Quinn's forehead. "They have been doing a full inventory review, so I'm guessing soon they'll know most of the things I've taken. So far no one has come to talk to me, so I think I'm still safe. How's she been today?"

"She's more relaxed but still has periods of restlessness. Her catheter showed some blood in the urine. Other than that, she's hanging in there."

Brian was relieved. He still wasn't over the scene from the night before when they had tried to wake her up. He prayed the next time would be easier on her.

"Morning," Brian called as he stopped beside Quinn's bed. "I've got to run into the hospital for a bit and then stop in and bug the detective. They had someone stop by yesterday to talk to me, but I want to keep bugging them, too."

"No problem." Greg assured him as he yawned. "We'll watch her and let you know if there is anything you need to know."

Six hours later, Brian was beyond ready to call it a day. Things were getting a bit touchy around the hospital, and he'd heard through the grapevine that a police report had been filed.

"I'm home." He called out as he entered the house and headed directly to Quinn. "How's our patient today?"

"We woke her up for a bit," Greg said in greeting. "The pain doesn't seem to be much better, so we didn't keep her up long. She squeezed my hand though."

Brian smiled and nodded at the news before turning to Christina and the look of trepidation on her face.

Christina sighed, "Well, when I bathed her, I noticed she'd flinched when I touched her skin. And when I tried turning her on her sides, it caused her heart rate to increase. Quinn has increased edema in her extremities as well." Christina wrung her hands as she looked at Brian. "And she's showing signs of organ rejection."

Brian dropped into a chair as his heart dropped at the news. He wasn't going to panic. She was going to be fine.

Brian was done. The hospital was too dangerous. He had to stay away. Unfortunately, that meant no more visits to the police, so it was a matter of time before they started looking for him.

Greg walked in, sipping his coffee. "How's our patient this morning?"

Brian rubbed his eyes. "Her fever is back, and she's not responding to the meds. She's taking more short, rapid breaths. Christina and I woke her up a couple of hours ago. She looked at me. I told her about the accident, but she's in so much pain still that we upped her pain meds again."

"Have faith. She's strong." He took another loud sip and left the room.

It was easier for Greg to say that. It wasn't his daughter in the bed.

Brian decreased the Brompton's and waited for her to wake up. Her eyes fluttering open was the most beautiful sight he'd ever seen.

"Dad?" Fear flooded her eyes.

"It's okay, baby. I'm here. There was an accident and you've had to go through a few surgeries. Are you in any pain?"

"It feels like someone is sitting on my chest. I'm so tired." She blinked slowly.

Brian kissed her forehead. "It's okay. Go back to sleep.

Christina opened the door. "We're done with her bath. You can come back in."

Brian rushed in. He had heard her crying through the door and it tore his heart out. "What's wrong? What hurts?"

"I don't know. My insides feel like they are being ripped apart. I don't want to do this anymore. Can you make it stop?" Large tears rolled down her cheeks.

Her words cut him deeply. How did he explain she was in pain because of what he did to her but that it would get better if she just fought a little longer?

It had been seven days since the liver transplant. He thought by now she'd be up walking around. Maybe even eating real food. She'd been so miserable they kept upping her pain meds, but nothing seemed to relieve her anguish.

Greg pulled a chair over next to Brian. "It's time to talk. Her heart rate hasn't gone below one fifty in two days. She's clammy and pale and is starting to give up."

Brian dragged his fingers through his hair. "I just

don't understand. Nothing makes sense. Those organs were healthy when implanted and all looked like they were working."

Greg sighed. "There's nothing left for you to change out. You've done vamp blood and shifter stem cells. Why don't you take her to Shifter General? Maybe they can fix her?"

Brian shook his head. "Didn't you see the press conference? They have everyone in the city, both human and paranormal, looking for me. If I walk in there, I'm immediately going to be arrested and that's assuming the hospital even lets us in since we're human. They aren't going to know she's got shifter organs and what can they do that we haven't done?"

"Then it's time to make her as comfortable as we can and let her die peacefully. Don't put her through anything else. It's over."

Brian shot to his feet. "Get out. I don't need to hear this right now. She doesn't need to hear this either."

Greg nodded sadly and left the room.

Brian leaned close to Quinn. "Don't listen to him. You're going to be fine."

The solid beep of the monitor pierced the room. "Greg, Christina. Get in here." Brian yelled in a panic.

He felt her neck, searching for a pulse. "I don't feel one."

Greg checked the other side of her neck. "I don't either." He dropped the head of the bed and started compressions. Christina ran to her head and bagged her.

"Brian, go to the closet. There was a defibrillator in the ambulance. I took it just in case."

Brian opened the case and handed Greg the patches while he turned on the machine. The monitor showed v-fib. The sound of the defibrillator charging filled the room. The device analyzed her rhythm and delivered a shock.

Brian choked on a sob at the sight of her body lifting off the bed.

The heart monitor changed from v-fib to normal rhythm.

"Her BP is low, but I think she's stable." Greg said as he took over bagging her.

They stared at the monitor, waiting to see if he was right.

Barely a minute had passed when she started having irregular heartbeats.

Brian squeezed her hand. "Quinn. Can you open your eyes? Look at me." He held his breath at her still face.

Christina grabbed his shoulder and tried to pull him back. "Let's take a walk. Give it some time."

He didn't want to leave, but staring at her unresponsive body was torture. But this was his penance. "You guys can take a break. I'll stay with her."

Four hours later, Greg and Christina quietly walked back into the room.

Greg studied the heart monitor. "It's been hours. Her rhythm is still unstable, and she's showing no signs of improvement."

"Brian..." Christina whispered.

He held his hand up. "I know, I know. It's time. Let me say goodbye to her, then I'll change clothes and we'll call an ambulance. You guys need to go before they get here."

He waited until they were out of the room before moving her arm and sitting on the edge of the bed. He let out a weary breath. "I fucked up Arlene. The day you left us, you made me promise to keep her safe, and I failed you, both of you. All I wanted was to help her grow up so she could be the amazing woman you knew she was going to be." He broke into sobs and laid his head on her chest. "If there is a God, I'm begging you, please take me instead of her. I've lived my life, I've done bad things. Take me and let her live. The world needs her. Arlene, if you are up there with God, can you please make him listen? Please have him save her. I'll do anything."

He stared at the ceiling like he expected to see Arlene, or even God, floating above them. He really had lost his mind.

He didn't move for a long time. He laid there, feeling her chest move up and down and trying to memorize her scent. "Okay baby. I know you're done."

He got up and grabbed his phone and dialed 911.

PART

Three

CHAPTER
Thirty-Two

MADDOX AND TRISTAN entered through the broken door. The four of them went room to room, making sure they were empty as they worked their way toward the sound of beeping. They paused with one of them on each side of the doorway, before going in yelling, "Hands up!"

"We're the only ones here. I won't resist. I've called an ambulance to come get Quinn." Dr, Rogers said as he raised his hands up in the air and stared up at the agents from where he sat beside the bed.

Maddox pulled out zip ties and secured him. Vic came in with the rest of his team. Everyone was silent for a moment as they took in the sight of the girl in the bed with machines all around and several full medical waste garbage bags in the corner.

Maddox helped the doctor sit back down. "So it was you from the beginning? You've always had Quinn?"

Brian sighed. "The hospital had given up on her, so I had to take matters into my own hands. Over on the dresser is a full report on everything I did. She is still dying and there is nothing else I can do. Please get her to a hospital so they can save her. I'll tell you everything. Just help her, please."

Vic turned to Detective Dickhead. "Can you go out and meet the ambulance so they know it's safe to come in?" He waited for the man to leave, then picked up the medical report. After a minute, he whistled. "I guess we don't need to ask what you did with all those shifters organs."

Maddox's head snapped around to look at Quinn. "You put them inside her?"

"I figured your kinds regenerative powers might be able to do what our human efforts couldn't do."

Maddox wanted to hate the man. He was a murderer, but seeing him so broken and hopeless made it easier to understand why he'd done what he did. Even if it was bat shit crazy.

"Paramedics are here," Tristan called as he moved to Brian's side. "I'll take him out so they have room to work."

Maddox pulled his phone out of his pocket. "I'm going to call Obinski and ask him to meet us in the emergency room."

When Maddox hung up the phone, Vic handed him the medical report. "You and Tristan go to the hospital. I want a report as soon as she's been evaluated. I'll have TPD take Dr. Rogers in for now and keep him in holding in case the hospital needs to ask him any questions."

Maddox nodded and went outside to find Tristan. "Come on. We're following the ambulance to the hospital."

Detective Dickhead took custody of Dr. Rogers from Tristan and led him to their police car.

As Brian was led away, he turned to holler at the paramedics bringing Quinn out. "She keeps going into v-fib. Watch her closely, please."

Maddox made his way back to the staging area to get his car. Tristan jogged up and climbed in. "The ambulance is pulling out now."

Maddox nodded. "How insane was that? I kind of expected to find the organs in like jars or something. I didn't actually think it would be a real Frankenstein situation."

"I feel like we should watch what we say from now on. We freaking called this one, didn't we?"

Maddox laughed as he followed behind the ambulance. "If the kid survives, I can't imagine what's going to happen to her. She's no longer human, but I'm not even sure if she's one of us either. Add in that she has to live with the knowledge her own father did this to her. That's one hell of a burden for a kid to carry."

"I hadn't thought of that. And I thought I had it bad." He trailed off as they pulled into the hospital parking lot and parked.

They made their way into the ER and quickly found Obinski waiting for them. "Here, you're gonna need this. Dr. Rogers kept meticulous records of what was done and everything that happened."

Obinski thanked Maddox absently as he skimmed the report. "This is insane." He muttered as he turned and headed towards the room Quinn had been placed in. "I'm going to transfer her to the ICU. We'll get her stable and do a CT to see what's happening inside her."

Maddox and Tristan followed them up to the floor and sat in the hall. Who knew how long it would take Obinski to have any answers.

Not long after, a nurse walked up and handed them a file. "We made copies of Ms. Rogers reports so you have the original for your files."

Tristan took them and thanked her.

Maddox yawned loudly for the tenth time. When he was sure his eyes were going to roll back in his head, the door to Quinn's room opened. They watched as Quinn was rolled out and pushed down the hall. Dr. Obinski walked over to join them.

"She's going for the CT now. I checked all of her incisions and everything is healed. It doesn't make sense for her to heal that quickly as a human. Her father's notes say he theorized the stem cells were helping with that and I tend to agree with him. I don't know the full extent of your case, but she had her liver, kidneys, and lungs replaced and wings added to her back." He paused and shook his head. "If those wings actually work, I'm going to be shocked. What he did was amazing actually and the scientific side of me really wants to see them function. Oh, and there's a note that after the lungs she developed gills on her neck. How amazing is this?"

Maddox looked at Obinski like he was crazy. Amazing isn't exactly the way he would describe it. "So if everything looks good, why did Dr. Rogers say she was still dying?"

Dr. Obinski shook his head. "At this point, I can't give you any answers. It's going to be a couple of hours before we get all the blood work and CT results back. After that, we should have a better idea of what we're dealing with. Why don't you guys go home and we'll reconvene in the morning? And if she takes a turn, I promise to call you right away."

Maddox nodded. "We'll call an agent in to sit here around the clock to keep the press away."

"Sounds good. Have a good night." Dr. Obinski took off down the hall.

Maddox looked at Tristan. "I think I would rather sit here than go back to the office. Can't we just let Detective Dickhead write up his report, then we just copy and change a few things? That would save a lot of time."

"And here I was going to say since you're team leader, you write up the report and I'd just sign yours. We were together for the whole thing, anyway."

"The shit rolls downhill. You do the report and I just sign it. Right, junior agent?"

"Not in this case. Senior agents always have to give the reports to their supervisors. For once I win."

"How about this, we'll do the reports together so it's done faster and then tonight I'll show you a tongue trick I haven't used on you yet." Maddox gave him a pleading look.

Maddox chuckled and left Tristan standing there

with his mouth open. Teach him to try to one up Maddox.

On the ride back to the office, Tristan flipped through the papers. "There's definitely more than one person's handwriting here. We know he had another man and woman helping him. Think he'll give them up?"

Maddox shrugged. "I doubt it. This was a purely altruistic act. He's not going to throw them under the bus." He tapped his thumb on the steering wheel to match the beat of the music. "I had a thought... if Frankenstein's monster was called Adam because he was the first of his kind, would she be Eve?"

Maddox pulled Scarlet into the driveway of his mother's house. "You know, before you came along, I was here maybe once a month. Now we're here twice a week."

"See, I'm a positive influence on you. At least that's what your mom told me."

"I really don't like that you have a private chat with my mom. What do you guys even have to talk about?"

"Besides you? All kinds of different things.

Shows we've watched that we think the other might like. She's been asking about going to visit my mom, too. I told her she could, because I'm not telling her no. But I worry if that's a good idea, though."

Maddox was impressed. "Wow. I didn't know she asked about your mom. That's pretty cool, actually. And don't worry about mom, she's a freaking ogre. A tiny human woman is no match for her. Honestly, the nurses would probably appreciate the help. But will they let her in? She obviously isn't human?"

"If they question her, she can say she has a thyroid issue." Tristan grinned and then shrugged. "I'll call them and clear it. I don't think they'd have a problem with it. They let me in without issue."

Maddox snorted. "Ten minutes after being there, I could see how hard their job was. They are probably grateful for anyone who visits. I bet they'd let a banshee in."

"If she ever shifted to foretell a death and started screaming, she'd probably end up killing a few others from fright."

Maddox and Tristan had tears rolling down their faces from laughing by the time they made it to the door of Marta's house.

Tallie opened the door and lifted an eyebrow at them. "What's so funny?"

Maddox gasped and then took a deep breath. "We were just imagining a banshee visiting someone in a senior center, then shifts to call a death and ends up scaring a bunch more to death."

"You guys are so messed up." She said as she stepped back and opened the door wide to let them in.

Marta poked her head into the hallway. "You're just in time. Silas is taking the steaks off the grill now."

"It's still weird to think of him being here." Maddox mumbled as he made his way to the dining table.

"Don't think about the bedroom, then." Tristan grinned.

Maddox gagged as he pulled out the chair at the end of the table.

"Sorry, you've been evicted. Silas sits there now." Tallie gave him a sarcastic smile.

"But this has always been my seat. I'm here and mom is at the other end." Maddox spun around to stare at Marta as she walked in with a bowl of salad. "You gave away my seat? The body's not even cold and you just replace me."

Marta rolled her eyes. "Sometimes you are such a child. Sit next to your man and be good."

Tallie smirked. "Which one of us is the sullen teenager again?" She questioned as she sat in her chair.

The object of Maddox's frustration waltzed in with the tray of steaks. "Evening. It's good to see you guys again." He walked around the table, putting a steak on each person's plate. He bent close to Maddox. "Don't worry, if you have a nightmare tonight, we promise you can still crawl into bed with us."

Maddox gagged again. "How am I going to keep my food down?"

"Since when have you had trouble keeping meat down?" Tristan winked as he cut into his steak.

Tallie laughed, "He's gagged twice in the last five minutes. I think you're overestimating his prowess."

Marta tsked at them. "Can we have a more pleasant dinner conversation?" She handed Maddox the bowl of green beans. "How's the case going with the missing organs?"

"And that's a more pleasant conversation?" Tristan gaped in shock. "This family is so weird."

"That's exactly why you fit in with us. No normal family would take you in." Maddox shot back. "But to answer your question, we actually closed our part of the case. We have the man who was taking the organs. It turns out his daughter was injured in the downtown attack and was dying. He took the organs to try to save her. Poor girl is barely eighteen. Mom died a couple of years ago. Dad is now going to jail for the rest of his life, and she is a hodge-podge mixture of human and paranormal."

"Is she going to survive?" Tallie looked stricken.

Tristan shrugged. "She's critical right now. We have her at Shifter General and we'll go back in the morning to get a full report and to find out what the medical plan is for her."

Tallie leaned forward. "What about when she gets out? Does she have any family?"

Maddox shook his head. "To our knowledge, there's no one else like her. It's not something to worry about any time soon though. She doesn't have much chance of beating this and even if she does, who knows how long recovery will take. They are doing their best but have no medical data to know survival rates or future issues."

Tallie's lower lip quivered. "That's so sad." She turned to Marta. "Can we take her in like you took me in?"

Marta gave her a small smile. "That's very sweet of you, honey, but I think it's way too early to be discussing something like that. I think we need to take it slow and see if she even survives."

Maddox smiled at Tallie. "It's very nice of you to think of that." Maddox glanced at his mom and saw her in a new light. He'd taken for granted how amazing she was. Between taking in Tallie and visiting Tristan's mom, it wouldn't surprise him if she took Quinn in too. Soon, he was going to end up with a whole bunch of adopted sisters. His life was so weird.

CHAPTER
Thirty-Three

"GUESS that didn't stay secret for long." Tristan groaned as they pulled into the hospital parking lot the next morning and saw all the reporters outside. "There is even a mix of human and supe channels standing side by side. That might be a first."

They headed into the hospital, yelling no comment as they pushed their way through the throngs of people and microphones. And he'd thought it was bad after his transformation and stay in the hospital.

"Obinski is up with Quinn. He'll meet us there." Tristan read the message as they waited for the elevator. "Hopefully, he's got some good news for us."

When they got to the floor, they saw a nurse

talking to him a few feet from Quinn's room. They stepped just out of hearing distance in case it was something sensitive and waited for them to be done.

When they were finished, Obinski joined them. "Morning. That's quite the zoo outside, isn't it?"

Maddox nodded. "How did they find out so fast? I bet it was Detective Dickhead who let it leak. Anyway, how's Quinn doing?"

Obinski sighed deeply. "I don't have good news. All the organs that were transplanted seem to be occasionally misfiring for lack of a better way to say it. We're checking her blood every eight hours and each time we get different results. With one test, her liver is perfect and the next it's failing. All the shifter organs are doing this. The organs that are hers, like her heart, seem to be perfectly fine. Although she is still having episodes of V-fib, we don't have a plan as of yet. We're trying to keep her stable and have been calling specialists around the world to get their opinions. This is groundbreaking, so we're a little lost. I'm going in for the next vitals check if you guys want to come in."

"I'd like to see her." Tristan agreed quickly. "I know our situations aren't the same, but I know what she's going through to an extent."

"I'd like to give her dad an update as well. I'm

sure he's desperate to know if she's okay." Maddox added.

Obinski nodded, "Of course. It might be good for her to hear people talking to her and encouraging her to fight and that she's not alone."

He opened the door and led them into the room. Tristan and Maddox pulled their weapons and pointed them at the man sitting beside Quinn, holding her hand.

"I'm not here to hurt anyone." Bryce Wilkinson, the dragon who'd been on the run, blurted. "I just needed to see her and tell her how sorry I am that this happened. I never meant for anyone to get hurt."

Tristan pulled Obinski behind them with one hand as Maddox moved forward. "Stand up and away from the kid."

Bryce laid Quinn's hand down gently and stood with his hands in the air. "I won't resist. I swear I don't want to hurt anyone."

Maddox holstered his gun and moved to restrain the other man. Once he was secure, they let him sit back down.

Bryce turned to look at Quinn as tears fell from his eyes. "Please, just hear me out. I want to help her. Dragons are the ultimate apex predator, right? We are at the top of the magical food chain. I heard the nurses talking about all the different kinds of organs she got. Maybe if you give her my organs, they will be strong enough to heal her. Maybe instead of a mixture of creatures, she can get better with all dragon parts?" He turned and looked up at Dr. Obinski. "Sir, I'll do anything to save her. There has to be something I can do to help her?"

Obinski sighed, "Mr. Wilkinson, you have to know we can't actually just take your organs like that. It doesn't work that way. And to be honest, even if we could, the chance she'd survive the surgeries is slim."

Maddox pulled out his phone. "I'll call Cole and have him come pick Mr. Wilkinson up."

Tristan smiled. "At least we'll have one of them off the streets."

Bryce gave them a big smile. "You can tell them to stop looking for the other guy. He was taken care of."

"I'll take him downstairs and wait for Cole." Tristan reached for Bryce's arm to escort him from the room.

"You know." Obinski called as he studied the Dragon. "He has a point, though. Dragon magic is the strongest of all kinds. Saying you're an apex got me thinking. What if that's the problem? She has multiple types of shifter organs. What if the issue is they're fighting for dominance? That's why sometimes the organ is good and sometimes they're bad. If you'd be willing to try, there's a chance that if we did a bone marrow transplant, it might be enough to dominate the rest."

Bryce nodded eagerly. "Anything. Just tell me what to do."

Maddox, Tristan, Cole, and the rest of the pod paced the small waiting room. Obinski said as soon as Bryce and Quinn were stable, he'd come give them an update. He had warned them that putting Quinn under anesthesia again was dangerous and there was a possibility she wouldn't survive the procedure.

Tristan was losing patience when the doctor finally walked in. "Mr. Wilkinson is stable and in recovery."

"And Quinn?" Maddox asked nervously.

"Considering Ms. Rogers was so critical-" Tristan's stomach dropped as he heard those words. "-it's a miracle that she is rebounding so quickly."

Maddox visibly wilted in relief. He had his hand

over his heart. "Jesus, you almost gave me a heart attack."

Dr. Obinski smiled. "Apologies. I didn't mean for it to sound that way. I'm happy to say she hasn't had any more V-fib episodes. Her color looks good, and she woke up and asked for a drink. We're just waiting for the bloodwork to come back to see if we see any improvement."

Maddox grabbed Tristan and hugged him tightly. "I don't know why I'm so invested in this, but I am so glad she's okay."

Epilogue

TWO WEEKS later

Maddox waited in the visitor's room for Dr. Brian Rogers to be brought in. He couldn't forgive the doctor for killing those shifters, but he felt he deserved to know how his daughter was doing.

"Agent, I'm surprised to see you here."

Brian looked like he'd aged a few decades in the couple of weeks he'd been in lockup.

"I wanted to give you an update on Quinn." Maddox waited for him to sit in the chair opposite him. "I wish it hadn't come at the cost of others, but you'll be happy to know Quinn is going to survive.

She's in rehab, but that's not expected to last much longer. Her body has healed remarkably fast.

"She's alive?" Brian asked. "I just need you to say that one more time, please."

Maddox nodded. "She's alive and doing well. She's going to make a full recovery."

Brian broke down into tears. "Thank you, thank you." He took a deep breath to steady himself. "Did you ever discover what the fight was about that started all this?"

"It turns out the minotaur was anti-human and planning an act of domestic terrorism. Mr. Wilkinson said the other man was on the way to set up the bombs when he caught up to him and tried to stop him. So, while what they did caused a lot of death and destruction, his act also saved a lot more lives."

Brian shook his head. "It really blurs the lines on good and bad, doesn't it?"

Maddox stood and moved to the door. He had nothing else to say to him and he wouldn't be back. He'd done his good deed for the year.

Four weeks later

Tallie skipped ahead and swung the front door

wide. Quinn walked through the door and looked around hesitantly. Maddox and Tristan followed her in, carrying several bags.

Marta and Silas walked out of the living room.

Marta smiled at Quinn. "You're already looking better than you did in the hospital. I'm so glad you agreed to stay with us."

Quinn smiled shyly. "Thank you for taking me in. I'm just so lost."

Tallie walked over and squeezed her arm. "It's going to be okay. We're here for you and I, for one, am thrilled to have another person in the house that knows who Harry Styles is."

Silas held his hand up. "Wait, I know him. He's great. He visits his parents in the Fae realm all the time."

Tristan watched them all talking with a smile. "What's next for her, do you think?"

Maddox shrugged, "Obinski will follow her care. We'll get her set up with someone to talk to her. She's going to need help dealing with it all. But she'll have all of us, so she'll be fine."

He leaned against the wall and watched his new family. They were their own version of a Frankenstein family and he wouldn't want it any other way.

The End

The agents of the Paranormal Investigative Services aren't going anywhere. Book three 'Taken Under Fire' releases June 8th, 2023 and will continue Maddox and Tristan's story.

About the Author

Cassidy lives in the Tampa, Florida area with her high school sweetheart, their three children, her dog Flynn who she loves obsessively, and her grand dog, Ryder. She loves reading and going to the movies. She also loves to travel and hopes to one day watch a baseball game in every MLB stadium in the country.

She also writes under the pen name C.K. O'Connor. Books by C.K. range from sweet romance to young adult to historical romance.

To learn more about C.K. / Cassidy please visit her online at

www.cassidykoconnor.com.

You can also find her on Facebook at

https://www.facebook.com/CK-OConnor-Author-101376192171379

OR

www.facebook.com/cassidykoconnorauthor

Hi, I'm Sheri Lyn. I live in Florida with the two loves of my life, my dog's Bailey and Boone. I love living here and couldn't imagine living anywhere else.

I'm an avid reader who kept dreaming of a story that wanted to be told and that's where my first book was born.

When I'm not reading or proofing, I'm at the evil day job where my sanity is tested on a daily basis. My sarcastic quips can provide a much-needed break until I can return home to my puppies and books, my joys in life.

Please visit my website to keep up with my books and to sign up for my newsletter for excerpts, give-aways, and fun.

Sherilynauthor.com and on Twitter - @sherilynauthor